The Officer

Eleven Science Fiction Short Stories

edited by Alasdair Shaw

First published 2017
ISBN10 0995511039
ISBN13 978-0995511033

Contents

Introduction

In 2016, I edited a sci-fi anthology entitled *The Newcomer*. It was pleasantly successful, so I decided to follow up with another.

As before, this collection of short stories was put together to showcase the variety of talented authors writing science fiction today. The eleven chosen come from around the world, each writing in their local variety of English.

Each tale presented here has an officer as its central character. Not all are military, but they all experience the range of conflicting emotions that come with the responsibility of command.

#

Dave is the officer in charge of Arancha Station's security. His sense of "Duty" to the job clashes with that to his family.
Underfunded and undermanned, his team struggles to keep the peace. When a bomb threat surfaces, Dave is forced to accept help from outside the security services, knowing it will come with a heavy price.

In "Patchworker 2.0", humanity is forced to live in domed centres as foul as the earth we destroyed. Artificial Intelligence holds the remains of society together, and a special team of Patchworkers keeps the AI functioning at peak performance.

Patchworker Evalyn Shore leads the investigation of a homicidal Artificial Intelligence that is taking over minds, leaving Patchworkers and AI managers as sacks of biomatter ready for the recycling bin. Can she create the patch to repair the AI? Or will it kill her first?

Gavin Dolridge has the worst job in the Kuiper fleet. His ship perpetually sails in orbit beneath Saturn, collecting space-junk and keeping an eye on the border of the Old Earth Empire. In between bottles of scotch, he babysits a crew of has-beens and a distant, solitary captain. The glorious life of an XO.

Officer Caspar graduated at the top of her class, but she's as green as they come. Now she's putting in her time doing a first tour on the junk ship, and it's all she can do to keep herself motivated when the mission means nothing and the commanders don't care.

But when the ship's computer starts acting funny and alarms begin to blare, action ramps up on the border, and Dolridge and Caspar find themselves in grave peril. Their ship is "Totaled". Can Dolridge confront the demons of his past to survive? Will Caspar rise to the challenge and get out alive?

Find your captain and bring him home. A simple order. That's why Viola's going to the trashy dive of a space station, the "Lucky Star".

The mission's supposed to be a simple get in, get out with Captain Morris in tow, but that's before a gambling debt and a feisty dealer complicate things. To get Morris back, Viola has to decide whether to play by their rules, or make her own.

"There Comes a Time" when the fate of humanity rests on one person's shoulders.

Warrant Officer Caris Elliot, the first Future Soldier, has only one mission: to find out why humanity will be wiped off the face of the Earth. But time isn't on her side.

Time travel technology mandates that wherever she is and whatever she's doing, she is snatched back to the present when her programmed hours are up. In the future, Caris has only her skills and wits to rely on.

Before Gladius Squadron, before being assigned to the ESV Winston Churchill, Capt. Jessica 'Aura' Davis was an Earth-based fighter pilot. In "Red Fortitude" she reports for off-world survival training on Mars, a new compulsory requirement for all UNE personal who wish to continue to climb the ranks, and the target of an unexpected terrorist attack.

In "Pithos", firefighters respond to a serious blaze. The building collapses and one of them is gravely injured. Can Doctor Mann's revolutionary device bring his son back?

In the far future, a tyrant's Empire becomes a civilised and decadent Commonwealth. Now nobles rule worlds in all but name. The Senate is a rubber stamp for the core worlds and the system staggers along. In the depths of space, alien races are watching and see a weak race, one that won't be able to hold onto their resources and star systems. Will the Commonwealth be strong enough to do what is necessary to win when the war comes? Can someone take "A Step on the Path" to salvation, or will countless billions of human lives be sacrificed on the altar of war by the aliens?

Young Marine platoon leader Jason McKay is forced to take his new command into a trial by fire, landing on a colony world torn by violence to free the hostages taken by violent revolutionaries. Will their "Rituals" save them?

In a post-apocalyptic society, where humanity's final bastion walls itself from surrounding zombie hordes, a rebel faction seeks to use the enemy virus as a tool for evolution. Gabriel Benson, right hand to the mysterious rebel leader known only as Green Skull, agrees to undergo the first genetic transformation, uniting human and zombie DNA to forge a new race. Among a gathered inner circle, he takes the injection of their fringe scientist's creation, becoming one of the "First Generation".

When the eight interstellar ships of the Diadem link up to the Necklace, Irina seizes the opportunity to land a new job on a new ship. Her extra height gets her a probational spot on the Aegea's peacekeeping force, and she's determined to make the most of it. The Aegeans are furious that someone is stealing their ceremonial fruit. Irina and her partner stake out their strange labyrinth in search of "The Grape Thieves".

Worries about making it through her probation are replaced by making it through the night.

#

And so, on to the stories. I hope you enjoy...

-o-

Duty

by Alasdair Shaw

A basket of oranges scattered across the corridor, bouncing orbs of colour against the monotonous grey of the station interior. Dave pushed a market-trader out of the way with one arm. The green-robed man sprawled over his stall and knocked more fruit to the floor.

^Suspect headed towards junction seventeen foxtrot,^ sent Dave as his feet pounded on the metal deck.

The blast door at the end of the corridor slid down, but not before his quarry ducked through.

Dave growled to himself and urged himself to run faster. ^Open it up again, he got past.^

The door began to rise as he reached it and he rolled underneath. He came up to one knee, sidearm pointed down the corridor, just in time to catch a glimpse of the thief as he disappeared round the corner ahead. ^Left at seventeen foxtrot. Tell me you've got someone between there and the Warren.^

Pumping his arms, he took up the chase again. He slowed for the corner, bringing his weapon up as he cautiously advanced.

^Negative. He's all yours, Sir.^

The thief was nearly at the entrance to the Warren. He glanced back as Dave closed the distance. The grin on his face showed he knew he had enough of a lead. Dave's hand twitched. He could shoot him down. No-one would see; the cameras on this level hadn't worked since he'd been assigned to Arancha Station.

Dave shook away the thought. Even after all these years, he couldn't stoop that low. ^Any luck identifying him from the picture I sent?^

^Not yet. Likely he's unregistered.^

A garbage robot trundled out of a side passage just in front of the fugitive. With a clatter of falling metal, he sprawled on the floor. He clawed his way back onto his feet but his ankle gave way and he half-collapsed, supporting himself on one of the knocked-over bins. He looked up and met Dave's gaze, the cocky grin replaced by worry and pain. He limped towards the entrance to the Warren and safety.

Dave lowered his shoulder and tackled him. They hit the floor and slid in the decaying rubbish strewn moments earlier. The thief struggled, but Dave knelt on top of him and managed to get hold of a wrist. He twisted the arm up, forcing the man's face against the deck. Pulling a set of restraints from a pocket, he cuffed his prisoner then pushed himself back, resting his back against the wall.

His chest heaved as he sucked down air. ^Suspect apprehended.^

^Well done, Sir. Officer Barcos'll be along shortly to help bring him in.^

Dave couldn't help wondering if they'd waited until he'd got the guy before bothering to task someone to help. He rolled his sleeve up and felt his forearm, finding a bruise forming.

The prisoner rolled onto his side and studied his captor. Some of his earlier arrogance returned to his eyes. "Ya can't touch me. I work for Mister Harrassa."

Dave narrowed his eyes. "I'd be very careful about making claims like that."

"Mister Harrassa looks after his family. If ya arrest me, he'll fill your world with pain."

"You sure?" Dave wiped sweat off his face with the back of his hand.

"Ya don't wanna get on his bad side."

"The thing is," said Dave, holstering his sidearm. "I happen to know you aren't part of Mister Harrassa's family."

The thief's eyes flickered sideways.

"I also happen to know that Mister Harrassa wouldn't take too kindly to someone pretending to be one of his own."

The blood drained from the thief's face. "You're... You're one of his men. Please. Please let me go. Don't give me to him."

Dave shook his head and stared at the floor.

#

Dave followed a muscular, suited man into an office. The bright, polished walls gave an idea of what the station had once been like, and gave him an overwhelming urge to check his uniform was tidy.

A middle-aged man in a white jacket and trousers stood before a ceiling-to-floor viewscreen, apparently admiring the savannah currently being displayed. He turned when the muscle coughed.

"Ah, Lieutenant Dave. So glad you could make it."

Dave tried to see him as a businessman, but couldn't keep the blood-stained images out of his head. "It's not as if I had much choice, Mister Harrassa."

Harrassa smiled. If he hadn't known better, Dave would have thought it kindly.

"Quite so, quite so." Harrassa indicated a cabinet. "Tea?"

"No, thank you." Dave swallowed. "Why did you ask to see me?"

"Straight down to business. I can admire that."

Dave was pretty sure he didn't want Harrassa's admiration. Having his attention was bad enough. Watching Harrassa pour boiling water into a teacup summoned up a memory of an autopsy on a badly scalded turncoat.

Harrassa sipped his tea. Lemon and bergamot wafted through the air. "I hear that you arrested a thief this morning. Quite an impressive chase, by all accounts."

"He wasn't one of yours," said Dave.

"Don't worry, I know. You're free to prosecute him."

Dave's mind and pulse raced. If that wasn't the reason for the summons...

"You know, Dave, I have a problem. There seems to have been a rise in unrepresented thieves in recent months." He held up a hand, forestalling Dave's response. "I'm not blaming you. In fact, after this morning, I think you can help me with the solution."

Realisation dawned, bringing with it a flush of relief. "You want me to remove your competitors."

Harrassa chuckled. "Oh, Dave. They aren't competitors. Their impact on business is inconsequential. It's a matter of principle."

At least this job would see him arresting real criminals, even if they were only low-level miscreants. "I'll see what I can do."

Harrassa placed his teacup reverently on the table then straightened. "Do I need to remind you what life on this outpost would be like if we weren't on the same team?"

Dave shook his head. When he'd first arrived, he couldn't make any arrests stick. Everyone closed ranks against him. Only after he accepted Harrassa's offer of patronage did he make any headway into the criminal world of Arancha.

Harrassa smiled warmly. "Of course I don't. I shouldn't have doubted your intelligence, Dave."

"I feel I have to warn you, it won't be a quick job." Dave studied Harrassa's face for any sign of a reaction. "I only have four officers."

Harrassa narrowed his eyes, staring straight at Dave. He nodded. "I understand. Perhaps I could lend you some of my men?"

"Thank you, but I'm not sure they'd be much help right now. I'd have a better chance of catching these guys if I continue to appear to be independent of you."

Harrassa laughed. "Appearances are indeed important." His face hardened. "But so are results. You have two weeks to show me you're up to the job."

Dave didn't dare ask 'what then?'

"Don't let me keep you any longer," said Harrassa. "I'm sure you're keen to be getting home. Maisie and George'll be back from school in a few minutes."

Dave's heart thudded and he swallowed back rising bile. He fought to keep a neutral expression as he left the office.

Outside, the muscle handed him back his sidearm. "The name's Frank. Mister Harrassa asked me to keep tabs on your investigation. Looks like we'll be bumping into each other more often."

#

"Breakfast, Maisie. Breakfast, George." Jessica placed a large bowl of fruit in the middle of the table and turned back to the counter.

She turned back with four plates of pancakes balanced on her arms.

"Let me get that for you, dear," said Dave, rising from his seat and reaching out.

Jessica carefully put a plate in front of each of the three empty chairs at the table, then plonked one in front of Dave. The syrup spilled over the edge and stuck to the tablecloth.

"If you don't hurry up, it'll get cold," she called.

"Urgh. Coming," said George. He emerged from his bedroom a moment later, hair sticking up on one side, pink-striped pyjamas dishevelled.

Dave rolled his eyes and cut up his bacon.

"Maisie. Now." Jessica poured three orange juices and placed the carton beside Dave's glass.

Maisie padded into the main room, tying her mauve dressing gown as she went. She hopped up onto a chair and picked up her glass of juice in both hands. Three big gulps later, she put it down and gasped.

George shoved a large piece of pancake into his mouth, hardly chewing before swallowing. "Screen, on."

Jessica scowled at him.

George sighed theatrically. "Got to watch the news, Mum. Project on the election for school due end of the week."

Jessica turned her glare on Dave. He held his hands up. "If he's got a project, he's got a project."

"Opinion polls suggest that Senator Jenkins is on course to be re-elected in the traders' vote," said a reporter on the screen.

"This is boring," said Maisie, looking around the table for acknowledgement.

"Whilst in the law enforcement vote, former Chief Constable Smith appears set to replace..."

Maisie threw her knife on the floor. "I want to watch Mister Piggy."

"You can't watch Mister Piggy." Jessica picked the knife up and wrapped it in a knapkin. "We're watching the news."

"Screen, play Mister Piggy." Maisie folded her arms.

"Screen, news. Lock," said Jessica.

Maisie screamed and pinched George. He shoved back, knocking over the remains of Maisie's juice.

An alert popped up in Dave's vision. With a groan, he put his fork down. "Sorry. Work. Gotta go."

"Really? You're just going to leave me to deal with this?" Jessica mopped the table with a cloth.

Dave grabbed his sandwiches from the counter and slipped them into a pouch. "It's the job."

"Why can't you do a regular eight 'til six job like other fathers?"

Dave steeled himself against saying something he'd regret. "Regular jobs don't come with a free apartment and a good school for the kids."

Maisie knelt up on her chair and put her head between George and the screen. George poked her in the ribs.

"Are we still on for lunch?" Jessica said, separating the children. "You haven't forgotten, have you?"

He reached his ID and sidearm from the wall safe and clipped them to his belt. "I'll call you."

#

Dave sauntered up to the crime scene tape, knackered overhead lights flickering in succession as if marking his progress. He nodded to Barcos and drained the last of the gritty coffee from his thermal mug. "Where's the body?"

Barcos flicked his head backwards. "In there. The doc's with it now."

"Do we know the victim?"

"Nope. Not a registered resident, and no record of him entering the station."

Dave ducked through the hatch behind Barcos. As his eyes adjusted to the gloom, he pulled up the compartment's access logs. No entries appeared for the last three standard days, until Barcos arrived, responding to an anonymous message.

"I'm putting the time of death six hours ago."

Dave looked around for the source of the voice, and found the doctor behind a grime-streaked table, kneeling under a large horizontal pipe. "Dammit."

The doctor looked up. "Not fit with your timeline?"

Dave shook his head.

^Sir? There's a crowd gathering out here.^

^Hostile?^

^Curious,^ sent Barcos. ^For now.^

"Looks like we might have to hurry this along, Doc." Dave

crouched beside her. "What else can you tell me?"

She pointed to a circular entry wound in the victim's forehead, the edges puckered and torn. "Probably a pistol. Note the stippling."

Dave peered closer. "Execution?"

"Looks likely." The doctor closed up her bag. "Let's get him back to the morgue."

Dave helped her lift the body into a bag. "Anything on the forensics front?"

"The blood's his. I didn't find anything else in the room. It wasn't even cleaned up, they must've used sealed suits."

"As usual." One of the biggest problems on a space station was the ease of access to suits which rendered most forensic tools useless. "Probably destroyed them too, so we won't even be able to match them to traces from here."

^Chan's here with the cart,^ sent Barcos. ^And the crowd's growing.^

Dave ducked out into the corridor and surveyed the gathered people. "Chan, Barcos. Go help the doc with the body.^

A familiar face caught his attention. Dressed in a worker's boilersuit and wearing a peaked cap, Frank held his gaze for several seconds before disappearing into the crowd.

"Fancy a lift back to the station?" asked Chan.

Dave turned to the two-person electric cart, with the body bag on a trailer behind. "No, thanks. I'm going for a walk to feel the streets."

Chan nodded. "Gotcha, boss."

"Want me to tag along?" asked Barcos.

"Nah." Dave glanced at the crowd. "Make sure the doc gets back to the infirmary OK."

Barcos nodded. "Will do."

The crowd broke up after Chan had driven off with the body and Barcos had walked the doctor to the nearest lift. Dave strolled along the corridor, vaguely heading for the market but letting his feet take him where they felt like.

A few junctions later, Frank stepped out of a shadow and fell into step beside him. "It wasn't us."

"It sure looked like a mob hit."

Frank tutted. "It doesn't do calling us the mob. Mister Harrassa's an above-board businessman."

"Whatever. This wasn't you?"

"There were no active termination orders. And no-one's movements are unaccounted for."

Dave skirted a bright orange puddle beneath a dripping, corroded pipe. "Could someone be trying to muscle in on business?"

"We'd know if they were. They'd leave a message, not the corpse of someone we don't know in a rarely-used utility chamber." Frank shook his head. "This suggests someone with an altogether different agenda."

Dave turned at the next junction and found a young boy in welfare-red clothes daubing something on a wall. He looked back, but Frank was nowhere to be seen. The boy's face was haggard, his fingers bony, and he didn't seem to notice Dave's approach.

Dave clapped his hand on the waif's shoulder, making him jump. "What you doing here, boy?"

The boy's eyes struggled to focus.

Dave looked at the crude Separatist symbol smeared on the wall in white paint. "How much they pay you to do this?"

The boy twitched his head.

"How about I give you some food for you to stop?" He pulled his lunchbox out of a pouch. "Beef and mustard roll?"

The boy's eyes locked onto the sandwich. He reached out slowly then snatched it, like a feral creature unsure about being hand fed. He took a bite then ran off, clutching the food to his chest.

One deck down from the market, in a corridor with few working lights, a man saw Dave and hastily stepped into a lift. Against a wall leant a woman wearing only a micro skirt and pair of boots. Red and gold swirls covered her skin, artistically highlighting her narrow waist and perky chest.

She lit a perfect smile and winked. "You going to book me, or hire me, officer?"

"Neither," said Dave, transferring a network address to her datapad. "Just give you the number of someone you can call. If it ever gets too much."

He took the lift up and stepped out into the market. A wall of noise, colour and smell hit him. Foodstalls offering cuisines from across the Republic took up every available space between the larger trading establishments. He sauntered through the crowds, catching snippets of conversations, reading the mood of the populace. Everything seemed as it should. Apart from a nagging worry in the back of his mind. If Harrassa hadn't ordered the hit, who had? And why?

#

Dave strolled into the station and hung his jacket on the wall by his desk. He settled into his fake-leather chair and loosened his collar. A drunk rattled on the bars of her cell, eliciting protestations from her neighbour who was obviously well on the way through his hangover.

Barcos got up from his desk and pulled a seat up in front of Dave's. "Thought you'd want to see the reports from the morgue. Cause of death's a no-brainer."

Dave took the proffered pad and skimmed through the autopsy report. The cause of death, gunshot wound to the head, was confirmed. He glanced up at Barcos, attempting to decide if the no-brainer comment had been deliberate. The doctor noted several old injuries, including several broken bones, two knife wounds, and a thermal shotgun hit to the abdomen.

"Somewhat of a fighter, our victim," said Dave. "Ex-military?"

"Not showing on any database we've got access to," replied Barcos. "But that's not the best bit. Check out the trace report."

Dave flicked across to the document detailing the analysis of substances found on the body. His eyes widened. "Explosives residue?"

Barcos nodded. "I checked it out. He's been handling some pretty potent stuff. A few hundred grams of that in the right place could breach a blast door."

Dave leant back, the wood-effect frame of his chair creaking. "What's their target?"

"I don't know."

"What?" Dave looked up. "Oh, sorry. I was thinking out loud."

"Could be a heist. There's plenty of valuable merchandise in dealers' strongrooms."

"True."

"Or sabotage. A covert Congressional attack, or someone with an axe to grind," suggested Barcos. "They could cost the outpost thousands a week by taking a docking tube out of commission. They probably killed the bomb-maker to tidy up a loose end."

Dave gave voice to the fear inside him, speaking calmly and slowly. "We could have a terror cell active in the outpost. The target could be anything that would give them publicity for their cause."

#

Dave wandered through the Park. An entire level on Arancha Station was given over to this green space, and another below to handling the irrigation and other support requirements. It formed part of the station's atmospheric processing system, as well as being home to several farms growing real food for high-end customers.

The area Dave was in was one of the public recreation areas. People ran and played all around him, couples relaxed on the manicured grass, children chased each other through undergrowth. Trees arched overhead, glowing animated signs for all sorts of products and services hanging from their branches. He stopped at the base of one tree and studied the screen embedded in its trunk. A reporter talked enthusiastically, waving his arms around; the caption below related that Fleet was mobilising a task force to meet a new separatist threat. Dave reached out and tapped a few commands, displaying the datestamp on the report. It had been filed two weeks previously, only now reaching Arrancha Station.

He walked on. The bonded rubber-crumb path curved round a fountain, its jets of water lit a kaleidoscope of colours by submerged lamps. On the far side, his wife sat in the middle of a bench, watching a shark-shaped balloon that swam through the air, covered in strobing adverts. To one side of her sat a bearded man in a casual jacket.

Jessica's eyes met Dave's and she stood and waved. He waved back. She smiled as he sat down beside her. He couldn't remember the last time she'd smiled at him when the kids weren't watching.

"You came," she said.

"I said I would."

"You've promised things before, but work..."

The man on the other side of her coughed.

"I'm sorry." Jessica leant back. "This is Doctor Lasca. Doctor Lasca, my husband, Dave."

"Glad to meet you, Dave."

Dave stared at the fountain. "What happens now?"

"Well, that's up to you." Lasca scratched under his chin. "You've already made the hardest step by seeking counselling."

#

^We caught a break, Sir,^ sent Barcos.

Dave continued perusing the shimmering fabrics on a stall on the market level. ^Go on...^

^I finished reviewing the security footage,^ sent Barcos. ^As you guessed, there were no working cameras covering the room or the hatch. But both ends of the corridor were covered. The camera at one end was panning, so there are gaps where someone could have got through unseen, but it's a start.^

Dave ran a gossamer-thin, iridescent scarf through his hand. George would love it. ^Excellent.^

^I ran everyone through the database. Chan and Singh have been running down the alibis for those we could ID, everyone has checked out so far.^

Dave transferred a couple of credits for the scarf and tucked it into a pocket.

^I was able to track the three men we couldn't ID,^ continued Barcos. ^Two are somewhere in the Warren. The other's on level three.^

A tall woman with a tray of flashing toys accosted him. He smiled at her and cast an eye over the gadgets. Maisie had a thing for tacky gifts.

^Good work. You got a specific room on level three?^

^Yep. Sending it to you now. It's registered to a woman and her three-year-old son. No mention of a man.^

Dave apologised to the toy-seller and hurried to the nearest lift. ^Meet me there.^

Barcos was waiting at the end of the corridor when he arrived. "No-one else was available, Sir."

Never a dull moment, eh?" Dave shrugged on the body armour that Barcos offered him, and drew his sidearm. "Ready?"

Barcos nodded.

"Go."

Barcos led the way along the corridor at a gentle jog, thermal shotgun pointing at the suspect's door. Dave stayed behind him, the pair presenting as small a target as possible. When they reached the apartment, Dave pressed himself against the wall alongside it, and Barcos stood across the corridor, still training his shotgun at the blistered paint of the door.

Dave checked Barcos was watching then banged on the door with his fist, keeping his body to the side. "Security! Open up!"

He thought he could hear chairs scraping across the floor. "Stand away from the door! We're coming in!"

He sent his override code to the access panel and the latch clicked off. A firm push with his hand and the door swung open. Barcos went in first. Dave followed a step behind, scanning every corner of the room. Two adults stood by a table with their hands up, a small boy hugged the man's leg. Steam curled up from several bowls of rice on the table. Dave's stomach gurgled, reminding him that he'd given away his lunch.

He covered the people with his sidearm while Barcos cleared the bedroom and the washroom. The woman and child matched the pictures on file. The man stood in front of them both, hands held out protectively. There was something of him in the boy's face. Dave crossed off the possibility that the man was holding them captive.

"No-one else here," said Barcos. "And no obvious weapons."

"Thank you, Officer Barcos." Dave holstered his sidearm then smiled and waved his hand to the table. "Please, sit down Mister and Missus Kym."

The woman hugged her son closer. The man looked from Dave to Barcos and back to Dave.

"It's all right. I'm pretty sure we've got the wrong address. We'd just like to ask you a few questions to be sure."

The room seemed stuffy. Dave checked his safety badge. The carbon dioxide level was high; not dangerous, but uncomfortable. He looked around the room, registering a few things that could be heirlooms, but nothing of any value. The apartment's environmental control panel was beside the door, and he set it to full scrub. The woman's eyes widened.

Dave walked the couple of paces to the table and sat. "As this is an official visit, none of the CO_2 extracted from the apartment during our time here will be chargeable to you."

Mrs Kym's mouth dropped open for a second, before she bowed hastily and sat, tugging on her husband's sleeve to get him to sit too. "What is it you want to ask?"

Dave stuck his tongue out at the child. He hid behind his father, but peeped back out again with a giggle. Barcos leant against the work surface that divided the cooking area from the eating area.

"We're just talking to everyone who was in Section Twelve

Bravo last night," said Dave. "Finding out if they saw anything unusual."

The couple paled and looked at each other.

"We're not interested in how you came to be on the station, Mister Kym. Nor how you're earning enough credits to feed your family without appearing on the tax roll. All I need is to be able to confirm your exact whereabouts between midnight and three this morning."

Mrs Kym poked her husband. "Tell him where you go."

He stared at the table. "I work shifts at a... club. Cleaning."

"What sort of club?" asked Barcos.

Dave scowled at him.

"An... exotic one," said Mr Kym, his voice almost a whisper. His wife shuffled away from him a fraction, face reddening.

"Can anyone verify this?" asked Dave, inwardly cursing Barcos' lack of subtlety. "A manager, perhaps?"

Mr Kym pulled a communicator out of his chest pocket. He tapped a couple of times then turned it to show Dave a network address.

^Chan? Could you check Mister Kym's alibi for me? He claims to have been cleaning at a club,^ sent Dave.

^Go ahead.^

Dave sent the address.

^Got it. I'll get back to you...^

"Where you from?" Dave held his nose and popped his ears. "Sorry, sometimes I struggle to equalise."

"We're from Jamary-Seven." Mrs Kym passed a handful of rice to the child, who shovelled it into his mouth.

Dave winked at the boy. "Why'd you leave?"

"It's one jump away from Ixus. People are divided between supporting their bid for independence and affirming their support for the Republic."

"Sounds like interesting times."

Mrs Kym shrugged. "Interesting times don't tend to be very safe for people at the bottom like us."

^Alibi checks out,^ sent Chan. ^Shift manager and bartender both confirmed seeing him at the club.^

^Thanks.^

"I understand. You won't get any grief from us about your residency or work status." Dave pulled a face at the child, then rose.

"Your alibi checked out. I hope you understand we had to check."

"Of course," said Mrs Kym.

Barcos sauntered out the door. Dave followed, turning back in the entrance passage. "Thank you for your patience. I'm sorry to have troubled you."

He closed the door and released his override on the lock.

"It's not him, then," said Barcos, slinging the thermal shotgun over his shoulder.

"No. Which means the perp's probably holed up in the Warren."

"We'll never catch him, then. Five of us against how many hundred? There's a reason we don't patrol in there."

The thought of people plotting to detonate a bomb on his beat ate at Dave's inside. He couldn't abandon the investigation. Two principles vied for supremacy in his heart. In the end, he knew which one he had to give up. "We could call for reinforcements."

Barcos laughed. "You never even got the stun rounds you asked for. They'll never send more cops in time."

Dave ran his fingers through his thinning hair. "I was thinking of asking someone closer to home."

#

"It's a terrible business," said Harrassa, reclining in a soft chair. He flicked his arms out to the sides, adjusting the shirt cuffs, then stretched them behind his head. "Very bad for takings."

Frank leant against a desk in the corner of the office, filing his nails.

"So, I decided to take you up on your offer of help," said Dave. "I can't search the Warren with the resources at my disposal."

Frank looked up. "Word has it a small-time Jazz dealer just stepped up a league. Got outside money. Might be worth dropping in on him."

"I thought you controlled all the drugs on this station?"

Harrassa coughed.

"Firstly," said Frank. "Accusations like that aren't helpful. Secondly, as you know yourself, exerting complete control over the Warren isn't worth the expense it would require."

Dave narrowed his eyes. "How do I know this is related to the bomb threat? That you're not just using me to make a problem go away for you again?"

"It's not exactly as if you're the one with the power down there.

If we hadn't told you, you wouldn't even have known there was a problem." Frank resumed filing his nails.

"Let me remind you of our little arrangement," said Harrassa, leaning forward. "You get to prosecute certain criminals. In exchange, if I ask you to deal with a problem, you deal with that problem." He held Dave's eye contact for a couple of seconds then settled back into his chair. "In this case, however, we're inviting you as a courtesy. Seems that dealing with this situation is in both our interests."

#

Dave led the team into the Warren. Eyes burned into him from the shadows, but no-one emerged. The twenty heavily-armed mobsters following him probably had something to do with that. After two junctions, the layout stopped resembling the plans in Dave's EIS. He stopped and looked around. Squinting, he could just make out cut-marks and welds.

"The guy we're after should be this way," said Frank, taking the lead.

Dave followed, noticing more evidence of the changes made since the Warren had been declared out of bounds a few decades ago. He'd studied the history of the station after accepting the job, and had wondered why none of his predecessors had ever reclaimed it. Then he'd arrived and discovered how few of Arancha's security personnel actually existed in real life.

The route twisted and turned, often squeezing past obstructions built into the corridor. Everyone they met made a big show of not seeing them. Dave got the impression that no-one saw anything down here.

"Just through here," said Frank. "Best you let me do the talking."

They ducked under a blast door, wedged half-open by an oil-streaked cart. A small boy sat against a wall, knees tucked up under his chin. His hand moved towards a box by his side, but then his eyes locked onto Dave. A smile cracked his dirty face, and he jumped up, scampering past the men and leaving the box behind.

Frank crouched and lifted the lid with the muzzle of his pistol. "Comm unit. Guess he was supposed to warn them." Frank looked up at Dave. "He seemed to know you."

"I gave him a sandwich this morning."

Frank chuckled then pointed down the corridor. "It's at the end of here then left. Two doors along."

Dave nodded and drew his pistol. "Remember, this is a security operation. I go first. No-one shoots until I've identified myself, and then only if they shoot at you."

The mercenaries griped amongst themselves, until Frank glared at them.

Dave paused at the end of the corridor and listened. A pipe dripped somewhere, but nothing else. He glanced back at his unlikely strike team and it occurred to him whether Harrassa lending them was a not-so-subtle way of reminding him who had the firepower on this station.

He held his left hand up, then counted down the fingers. On reaching zero, he made a fist and stepped round the corner. Soft footsteps followed him as he smoothly approached the target door. The chances of his override working down here were so miniscule he didn't even try, instead attaching a lock-breach box. He stepped back and triggered it with a thought through his EIS. It flashed and clanged to the floor, a neat circle of door held in its grip. Frank grabbed the door, pulled it open, and chucked in a couple of stun grenades.

Twin bangs rang out and brilliant white light flashed round the doorframe. Dave stepped through the gap, weapon up. "Security. Nobody move."

He scanned the room, heart pounding. It was empty of people, and almost anything else, apart from a table and chairs. Several mugs sat on the table, surrounded by food wrappers.

The rest of the team poured in after him. They moved professionally, covering their arcs and avoiding conflicts as they cleared the suite of rooms.

"What have you been training them for?" he asked Frank, then realised he probably didn't want to know the answer.

"Protection." Frank shrugged. "They're all ex-military anyway. It's not as if we're running a boot camp."

The last pair reported clear and Dave holstered his pistol with a heavy heart. Their one lead, and they were too late. He felt a mug of coffee with the back of his hand. Stone cold; they had a decent head start too.

"You should see this," said one of the mercenaries.

He led them to a larger room in the suite. A table at one end was covered in bits of electronics. The wall above it had a map of one floor of the station.

"You think the target's on that floor?" asked Frank.

"Possibly. It's one of the main public areas. Lots of potential targets."

He scanned around, looking for anything else.

One of the mercs returned carrying a pad with a broken screen. "Found this in a pile of smashed up hardware."

Hope sprung up. Dave smiled. "I'll take it back to the security centre. We've got routines that should be able to access it."

"Why wait?" asked Frank. "Hattie. Get in here."

A short woman with spiky black and red hair came through, slinging a thermal shotgun to her side.

"Reckon you can do anything with this?" Frank held up the pad.

Her eyes lit up and she cracked her knuckles. "You know I can."

She dumped a bag on the table and pulled a device out of it which she connected to the pad.

"What's she? Some sort of hacker?" Dave whispered to Frank.

"Digital security expert," replied Frank.

"Ah, right."

"The storage array is physically damaged, but I've connected directly to the individual nodes." Hattie's eyes defocused. "Let's see what they had on here."

Her fingers twitched and a tic developed on her left cheek. After a few seconds, her eyes refocused and she grinned. "Amateurs."

"What?" asked Dave.

"They deleted everything before they smashed it."

Dave struggled to reconcile her smile and her words. "Isn't that a bad thing for us?"

Frank placed a hand on his shoulder. "Hattie's rather an expert on recovering lost data. People leave all sorts of useful stuff on their devices."

"Looks like they were making fake voter identification cards. There's also a record of them hacking the registration system. Can't tell you what they accessed, I'm afraid, but I'd speculate they inserted records to match the ID cards."

"Any photos or names to go with those cards?"

"No such luck. They must've been on the nodes I couldn't repair."

"You have your target," said Frank.

Dave swallowed. "I had hoped it'd be a heist. Not terrorism. I don't have the resources to deal with this."

"You've got us," said Frank. "Mister Harrassa was quite clear that I was to take this outfit down. They're bad for business."

#

Dave pulled a loose-fitting beige shirt over his body armour and checked he could still reach the pistol strapped to the small of his back. Barcos strode into the cramped changing room and dropped his kitbag on a bench.

"We didn't find anything in the sweep," said Barcos, shrugging off his uniform jacket. "No bombs, no surveillance that wasn't ours, no evidence of tampering at all."

"So, the polling station might not be their target." Dave put a foot up on a bench and fastened his shoelace. "Or they're going to try to walk it in during the day."

Barcos pulled on a pair of grey casual trousers. "I left Chan guarding the entrance. Santiago and Pritchard are being as visible as possible elsewhere on the station, to stop them thinking we're concentrating here."

Dave swapped feet. "Good. I take it the chemical sniffer's working?"

"The portable one isn't modern enough to detect the explosive we know they're using. So I stripped the sniffer out of that passenger airlock that had to be refitted a couple of years back."

"The Dockmaster give you any grief?"

Barcos put his arms through a long mustard-coloured jacket. "I didn't ask him."

Dave laughed. "That'll come back to bite you. Just you wait."

They finished getting ready in silence. Dave reviewed the upcoming operation, trying to get his head round all the possibilities.

Barcos sat on the bench next to him. "You could have told me, you know."

"Told you what?"

"That you were working with Harrassa. I wouldn't have judged."

Dave sighed. "How'd you find out?"

"You started getting results. I've been around long enough to know there's only one way that works."

"Well, as it happens, I was going to tell you now, anyway. You need to know that we've got backup today. Harrassa's private army."

Barcos looked up. "That's real? I mean, I'd heard rumours..."

"Bunch of former Marines and soldiers. Very effective team."

Barcos sighed. "Guess that means we've got no chance of taking him down."

"Not by force." Dave rolled his shoulders. "But this is a discussion for another day."

The pair left the security centre and made their separate ways to the polling station. Dave avoided making eye contact with Chan as he shuffled through the entrance following a group of young women draped in tinsel.

The hexagonal auditorium rang with loud conversation. Scores of people mingled, chatting and eating. Looped recordings of the candidates covered all six walls. A row of polling officials sat at tables in front of the voting booths, checking polling cards against their records before allowing people through to the tall red cubicles.

Dave lingered for a while, buying a fruit blend with a paper umbrella in it and sipping as he wandered around. After a few minutes, he caught a glimpse of Frank leaning against a foodstall. They studiously ignored each other; no point risking getting made. He continued to circulate, making small talk with a few people on the way.

After an hour, Dave approached the polling officials. He presented his card and waited while they pulled up his image on their screens. They gave him a token, which he took to the booth and inserted in the reader. It chimed and lit green, then invited him to stare at a red dot. A flash, and it had checked the pattern of blood vessels on his retina. The candidates in the law enforcement vote appeared on the screen. Dave tapped Candidate Smith's image and then confirmed.

Leaving the booth, he did another slow lap of the auditorium. Part-way round, he bumped into a middle-aged woman in a smart green suit.

"Sorry," he said, bending to pick up the pamphlet she'd dropped. "Oh, hello, Mrs Jones."

"Er, hello... Just a minute... Maisie's dad?"

Dave wiped his hand on his trousers and reached out to shake hers. "She talks about you all the time. Loves your lessons."

Mrs Jones blushed. "Why, thank you. Always nice to hear."

"Having a nice day?"

"Oh, yes." She peered over his shoulder and waved. "Ah, there're my friends."

Dave inclined his head. "Don't let me keep you. Have a good day."

He checked in with Santiago and Pritchard. Neither had run into anything out of the ordinary, so he suggested they made their presence known on the main market level. His stomach rumbled and he headed for a foodstall.

One of the candidates displayed on the wall launched into an impassioned speech. The subtitles flowed fast, all about dignity and respect for tradition.

A woman's shriek filled the auditorium. Dave span round, drawing his pistol and exposing his badge. People ran across his view. He pushed his way towards the source of the commotion. A boy, barely older than George, stood with an arm round Mrs Jones' throat and a ceramic gun to her head. The crowd pressed towards the exit, where Chan tried to keep order.

A burst of gunfire came from outside the auditorium. Chan went down, crumpling against the wall. The panicked voters crushed together like sheep circled by wolves.

Off to one side, Barcos leant against the upright of a foodstall, weapon trained on the hostage-taker. Frank drew his own pistol and said something into his wristpiece. He advanced on the entrance. The two officers on patrol elsewhere confirmed they were on their way.

Automatic weapons-fire erupted in the hallway. A young woman stepped backwards into the auditorium, firing a carbine along the corridor the way she'd come. Frank raised his weapon and put a bullet in the back of her head.

The gunfire eased. A man crawled into the room, dragging a bag. One limp leg left a wide smear of blood on the floor. He reached into the bag. One of Harrassa's mercenaries stepped in and fired two shots into his forehead.

More mercenaries followed, setting up a perimeter. Frank peered into the bag. A message popped up in the corner of Dave's vision. <<Explosives, and a manual trigger.>>

Two of Frank's men beckoned to the civilians.

"Nobody move," shouted the boy with a gun to Mrs Jones' head.

Her eyebrows went up as the boy squeezed her throat. Dave locked eyes with hers, willing her to remain calm.

The boy looked up at the camera in one corner of the auditorium.

"This is happening because the Republic has not recognised the independence of Ixus."

^Boss?^ sent Officer Santiago. ^I'm on your level, but I can't get to you. There's a bunch of mercs outside the polling station.^

Dave cursed himself for risking a friendly fire incident by not passing the information. ^It's OK. They're the good guys. For today, at least. Check on Chan.^

"We tried through the courts, we tried peaceful protest, but it fell on deaf ears." The boy glanced at Barcos and then Dave, before looking back at the camera. "Now we have only violence to make ourselves heard."

Another message from Frank popped up in the corner of Dave's vision. <<One of my guys has a shot. Should she take it?>>

<<Negative.>>

The boy raised his voice further. "This will keep happening until the Republic sees sense. Your leaders could have stopped this. The blood is on their hands."

"What's your name?" asked Dave.

The boy frowned and looked at Dave. "I am a Child of Ixus. That's all that matters."

"I was just wondering, I've got a son about your age. My name's Dave, by the way."

The boy flicked his head as if trying to dislodge a bee. "You're just another representative of the oppressors."

Dave sighed. "Listen. There are two ways this ends. Either you let Missus Jones go and walk out of here with me, or I shoot you. I don't want to have to do all the paperwork shooting you involves."

"I came here knowing I would die." He shifted his grip on the gun.

^Chan didn't make it,^ sent Santiago. ^And Pritchard's here too. What do you want us to do?^

^Stand by. Don't let him see uniforms.^

"What subjects are you studying at school?" Dave smiled. "My son's studying history, politics, and philosophy."

The boy's eyes refocused and his shoulders relaxed a fraction. "I was doing history too. With exobiology and atmospheric science."

"That's a handy combination. Lots of good jobs in those fields."

"That's what my mum said. She was keen for me to join a colony prospecting..." The boy tightened his grip on Mrs Jones' throat. "They warned us about this. Negotiators trying to 'make a connection'."

Dave's stomach sank. He took up the slack on his pistol's trigger. The boy looked up at the camera again. Dave squeezed the trigger. The weapon kicked in the heel of his palm, the force absorbed by his arm muscles.

The boy's head went back and his arm slid away from his captive's neck. Barcos fired twice. The boy's body collapsed to the floor. Mrs Jones stood, muscles locked, eyes wide. Dave swallowed down bile.

The rest of the civilians ran for the exit. Two of Frank's team, rifles slung behind their backs, hurried them through; the rest stood alert, weapons ported.

^Help the mercs process the civilians,^ Dave sent to Santiago and Pritchard. ^There might be another separatist hiding amongst them.^

Barcos ran over and checked the boy. He holstered his pistol. ^Dead.^

Dave held an arm out to Mrs Jones. "It's OK. He can't hurt you now."

#

Dave waited in the corridor for five o'clock. Most of the paperwork was done, what was left could wait until tomorrow. The school doors opened and scores of children rushed out. Dave watched intently.

George stopped in his tracks. "Is everything alright, Dad?"

"It is now." Dave ruffled his son's hair and put his arm round his shoulders. "Come on. Let's pick Maisie up then get ice cream on the way home."

George frowned. "I'm not sure Mum would be happy about us spoiling our teas."

"I called her. She's meeting us there."

"Are you and Mum OK now?"

Dave looked at George. "It's a start."

-o-

Alasdair Shaw grew up in Lancashire, within easy reach of the Yorkshire Dales, Pennines, Lake District and Snowdonia. After stints living in Cambridge, North Wales, and the Cotswolds, he has lived in Somerset since 2002.

He has been rock climbing, mountaineering, caving, kayaking and skiing as long as he can remember. Growing up he spent most of his spare time in the hills.

Alasdair studied at the University of Cambridge, leaving in 2000 with an MA in Natural Sciences and an MSci in Experimental and Theoretical Physics. He went on to earn a PGCE, specialising in Science and Physics, from the University of Bangor. A secondary teacher for over fifteen years, he has plenty of experience communicating scientific ideas.

You can continue to explore the Republic and Congress in the Two Democracies: Revolution series.

Homepage: **http://www.alasdairshaw.co.uk/twodemocracies**
Mailing List:
http://www.alasdairshaw.co.uk/newsletter/officer.php

Patchworker 2.0

by M Pax

Eyelids twitching, drooling like a simpleton, Carl lay on a gurney. I came to replace him, hoping not so exactly, and hugged my navy trench coat tighter. The October chill piped into the habidome, as if people still lived with the world, nipped deeper into my veins.

Carl and I had flirted with love back in the Academy, before becoming fully licensed in PO, *Patchworkers Order*. PO forbade our affair, threatening to send us back from where we came. No way would I return to craptacular Sludge Bay. Carl vowed he'd take a stroll outside rather than live in Solder Park again, which was located on the edge of the landfill. He swore the stink followed him. Sludge didn't smell any better. We put our blooming passions on hold and had planned to revisit them when we retired. Now that'd never happen.

The medtechs strapped up Carl's stocky arms so they'd quit flopping around and tucked away his disturbing empty state as readily as the city dome concealed the raging storms and scalding ultraviolet rays. Before they wheeled Carl toward the ambulance, I straightened the lapels of his trench coat and committed to memory a face so dear.

Most wouldn't call Carl beautiful. His cheeks mooned out with bulbous outcrops, a boulder-like nose and pronounced brow ridge. His fleshy lips, once brimming with pink verve and promises, matched his strong jowls and double chin.

Sighing, I scanned him. Interfaces, thin micro-patches of circuitry, covered my skin and Carl's like most people wore clothes. I should have sensed him before the rail car stopped to let me out. His thoughts should have mingled with mine during the twelve block walk from the station. I should have perceived him beyond what my fingertips could touch. Frowning, I lifted his sleeve and pressed the black-lined circuit inked on my wrist to the same on his.

"Carl, what happened?"

Seizures weren't uncommon for patchworkers, but none of those prone to them ever made it into PO. I detected no pain echoing through his tattoos and nothing of what made Carl the man he was.

PO let me tap into reports it had archived on this AI. Carl hadn't been the first patchworker put on the job. He had replaced Gaati and Kawana. They had also ended up like this.

Crap. Three patchworkers down. Now only one hundred ninety-seven people on the planet had the ability to patch into AI and manipulate the minds of machines. Our elite group could resist getting lost in the knotted streams of code when the things went haywire. We were the few that could distinguish biological and mechanical electrical pulses, the few that could make sense of them, the few who could create necessary patches.

I pressed my wrist to Carl's once more. All my interfaces strained to boost the signals, searching the data he had collected on this client. Into his main processors I hacked, swaying for a moment when I stared up at myself; tall and big boned, square-jawed, the telltale silver irises of a patchworker, and red ringlets flowing down past my shoulders. My curls fluttered in the gentle wind, which was piped through the dome's vents. The breeze had a curdled smell to it, some days worse than others. Today it reeked.

Carl's job logs ended the moment he arrived, as if erased. I found the same exclusions in Gaati's and Kawana's records. I didn't believe in coincidence. PO heard my doubt and sent an instant avowal that it hadn't deleted anything from the logs. Had the AI?

The repeated omissions gave me pause, and my second thoughts darted over the nearby gray door that had no signs or windows. It appeared so harmless. No advisories alerted my interfaces. Yet what lay beyond those doors had rendered Carl into a sack of biomatter ready for recycling. His skill level rose to a mere half notch below mine. Would I fare any better?

PO demanded I go meet the client, nudging my childhood memories until the fetid aroma of sludge filled my mouth. I needed no other incentive and ducked into the entrance.

Red diagonal stripes on the floor gave the briefest warning. Beyond them, a squadron of six Marines levelled assault weapons. Six red dots sprouted on my chest. None quivered.

Their aim gave me no choice other than to hold out my hands like a common hacker. "Patchworker Evalyn Shore. I'm expected."

The Marines didn't jostle, so I didn't see the suit taking cover behind them. I heard him, though. His voice, more shrill than the sirens outside, grated over my jitters like corroded code. "Patchworker Shore, you were scheduled to arrive twenty minutes ago."

The words flitted in my ears as a question rather than a demand. Peering around the burly soldiers, whom I matched in breadth and height, I sized up the peon sent to fetch me. A lack of authority sloughed off his cheeks like the dirty rain on the dome. I could smell his nerves, which added a sour note to the hard-used air.

"My orders are to answer only to Director Beatty. Where is he?" I brushed my red ringlets behind my ears and discreetly tapped my booster interface. The peon remained as unreadable as Carl.

"I'm Assistant Director Randall." He held out his moist hand. It trembled.

Lots of people contracted a case of the fidgets when meeting a patchworker. As I said, we were a rare breed, but this stooge had already met Carl, Gaati, and Kawana. He had to know the rule against touching patchworkers. If PO wouldn't reestablish my residence in Sludge Bay for bailing, I'd march back to the rail car right now.

Sweeping past Randall, I strode into the corridor leading to the AI. "Let's get ticking, bub. You now have me twenty-six minutes behind. I've a reputation and all. Run, run."

Despite my brisk pace, he fell into step beside me. The odd spongy texture of the ruddy brown tiles deadened any echo.

"Director Beatty and I are pleased you could come on such short notice," he said. "You were born in Sludge Bay, weren't you? What an inspiring rise in status."

Since he didn't matter to anything more than a defunct subroutine, I didn't bother to answer, and I was relieved he didn't continue to jabber. It was of no consequence which district a person had been born in if she or he had the ability to become a patchworker and a damned good one.

Perhaps this assistant director boy wanted to get me riled, riled enough not to notice the absolute void. Neither my interfaces nor my senses picked up anything other than lemon-scented cleanser and heavily insulated walls. Everything pinged back as a dead end. The minty-hued corridors zigged and zagged. The cushion of the ruddy tiles grew deeper, stumbling my steps. I found it harder to swallow.

A set of doors appeared on the left. Randall stopped in front of them. Silently he summoned them open using tech I couldn't detect. That had never happened. Warnings shivered down my spine. Randall shoved me inside.

Lined with blinking lights and hardware, the dim room buzzed and twinkled. The man standing in the middle of it all had to be Director Beatty. He stared blankly into space, unshaven, tie and jacket askew, fingers twitching. His tongue flickered at his dry lips.

In stilted steps, he pivoted, staring into my face. As if a circuit switching on, thoughts lunged at me, screaming, sniveling. The onslaught after total nothing shocked me. My knees buckled.

Beatty reached out to catch me. I veered sharply the other way to avoid his touch. A good number of interfaces could be lost by innocent contact, and his void expression creeped me out. It reminded me too much of Carl.

Boosting my sensors, I worked harder to scan him. Beneath the overwhelming chatter of AI in the room, I could make out Beatty's mind; overwrought, lost, fearful. I knew that much only because it had been allowed. By him or the machine?

"Ah, Mayflower has introduced itself." A ring of hair fringed his round head like a wire-rimmed screw hole on a circuit board. The top of his pink skull puckered with his words, emphasizing his nerves in the oddest way.

I amplified my connection to PO, checking to make sure my ability to communicate remained unobstructed. "We're here," PO whispered. Good.

I greeted the AI. It cooed so eagerly, inundating my conscious and unconscious thoughts, replacing my emotions with its own. Powering on the tattoos at my temples, I muted Mayflower's babble.

A machine should mind its place.

"Tell me the problem. Leave out no detail," I said to Beatty. His opinion and analysis mattered most. The human caretaker's assessments trumped all in extreme cases. This job definitely fell into the extreme category.

"My digital colleague is in need of something I can't provide. It knows you can."

A knot formed in my forehead, narrowing my vision. "How can you know what I can provide? And what happened to Carl? Gaati? Kawana? Any of them should have been able to fix your problem. They're as PO certified as I am."

"Only the best will do." His lips clamped tight together, and he gestured at the jack-up chamber, a soundproof room with jacks, interfaces, speakers, and monitors where I'd visit with Mayflower. The AI could manifest as a hologram in there if it wanted.

The AI gave me a mental push. I walled it off by setting the tattoos at my temples to maximum strength. The connection had to happen on my terms, and I communicated to Mayflower that I wouldn't budge until it demonstrated some courtesy.

It dialled down the aggression, giving me the space I demanded. Good.

To prepare for merging, I silenced communications from any source other than the AI and PO. Then I thanked Mayflower and accepted its invitation. Inside the chamber, I lay down, getting comfortable.

Before settling into a union with the machine, I set my anchors, boosting my connection to PO, isolating my personal processing chip, setting it to beep every three minutes, fixating on the cool draft blowing over my right hand chilling my fingers to ice. *Join with me, Mayflower.*

I need. I hurt.

The emotion in those simple words overpowered my defenses. Beatty, Randall, the weird facility, Carl, everyone and everything faded away. Mentally I embraced the AI, calling it friend. *Let me help you. Who named you Mayflower?*

Dr Navin. She created me.

Where is she now? Sometimes all it took was an understanding of who had authored the routines and subroutines. Few could resist imbibing their personalities into their AI.

My PO interface accessed the global library and fed me data on

Dr Navin. Her work involved evolution. Her biography didn't mention any programming credentials, and Mayflower didn't appear on her list of achievements.

Aboard.

For a moment I blanked, my thoughts sputtering. *You're a ship? To where?* Why hadn't PO given me this information?

PO claimed not to have known. It scanned the library files for a list of possibilities. Mayflower stopped the search when PO pinged over ERC 14, *Earth Reboot Candidate 14.*

I heard myself gasp. *Are you there now? Or is that the issue? You've run into a travel snag?*

I'm here. The mission can't fail, Evalyn. Would you like to see your future?

A new home on which to grow and start over would solve a lot of problems on Earth. The scope of Mayflower's mission wasn't lost on me. I had to fix this AI. *I'll help you succeed. May I see? I'd like to.*

That's a relief to hear. Now I feel better. Mayflower let me slip farther into its systems, cradling my consciousness, guiding me over the expanse between us. My stomach flipped.

At first, all I saw was white; the floor, ceiling, and walls. Consoles shrunk navigable space in the ship's operations center to three feet. The banks of machines hummed, working, winking, part of Mayflower. It took a moment to orient myself as to where I fit in and to discover my consciousness had entered a robotic explorer. I had treads and three metal arms. I rolled toward the nearest window.

Darkness spanned in every direction revealing nothing. Sadly disappointed, I prepared to amble off and explore the ship. An eerie purple flash stopped me. It illuminated the alien vista. Green. Gobs and gobs of green, as if the ship lay at the bottom of a strange ocean. The flashes continued, reminding me of an electrical storm.

Unable to tear away, I continued to peer into the exotic depths that flickered in and out of view. Aware ultraviolet and x-ray scanners had been built into the probe, I activated them. Some sort of bio mass drifted out there, phosphorescing with the tides and currents. After making an inquiry at the global library, PO pinged me with the nearest Earth equivalent, seaweed.

Its undulations hypnotized me, transfixing me to the spot. I scoured the green for a scrap of something more profound, for the salvation humanity so desperately sought. A tiny beep shook me from the window, reminding me of the job. As wonderful as it was to explore ERC 14, I couldn't help Mayflower if I became lost in its protocols. For added grounding to my body, I confirmed the frigid draft on my hand and exchanged hellos with PO.

Reconnecting with the physical world roused the robot me from the window. The ship was so quiet. Too quiet. *Where's your crew?* I said.

The mission records I could access informed me Mayflower had been outfitted with a crew of twenty to establish an off-Earth colony. The crew had to succeed. Had to. I tired of living inside a dome, tired of living on a planet that could no longer provide what people needed to survive.

They left, Mayflower answered.

All of them?

They went out there and didn't come back.

Did you send robots like this one after them?

Of course. They didn't return either. This is the last one.

I jacked deeper into Mayflower, searching for its communication logs. *Have you tried to raise them on comms?* The logs sat in front of me, but wouldn't open. *Mayflower, grant me access.*

I can't.

You can't communicate with them or you can't open the logs? Such an ambiguous answer struck me as strange.

Examining Mayflower's original directives, I could plainly discern Dr Navin's primary protocol, which charged the AI with a duty to safeguard the crew. The encrypted line of code with it suggested an overriding command to ensure success of the mission. Usually any superseding instructions required a specific crisis before becoming an AI's law. Had those circumstances arisen? Elaborate security measures encased the secret orders and wouldn't let me in, not yet. The chill on my hand in the jack-up chamber spread to my wrist.

I can't do either, Mayflower said.

My scanners discovered no programming issues with Mayflower's communications. I rolled the robot toward an access panel and checked inside. *This circuit is bad. I can fix it, but don't you have redundancies? Why didn't they take over?*

This mission can't fail, Evalyn.

The AI's worry tightened my stomach on Earth. For reassurance, I patted the ship's wall with one of my mechanical arms. *Don't worry. I'll get it on track.* Pliers and soldering iron in robotic hand, I repaired the module.

I had to instruct the system to reboot. While waiting for it to come online, I rolled through the vessel hunting for signs of the crew, seeking clues as to what had happened. My search only rooted out more questions.

Blankets on two of the bunks lay bunched. I imagined Dr Navin and the mission commander leaping up from a sound slumber, sprinting toward trouble. What kind had sent them running? In the tiny living quarters, three trays of food sat rotting in front of a monitor playing a movie, *The World To Be*, everyone's favorite about Earth restored. Did it play in a loop or had the crew just left?

On Earth, I tugged at my lapel. The robot me went to check the lockers. Empty. Not one spacesuit hung on the pegs. Not one helmet or pair of boots graced the shelves. Pivoting the robot's sensors around, I glanced toward the airlock.

If not onboard, everyone had to have gone out there. Had they found our new paradise? I headed toward the window, digging deeper into Mayflower's archives.

The speakers onboard the ship blasted to life. In the jack-up chamber, I jumped in my skin. The robot me merely shuddered to a halt.

"We're here, Mayflower. Send the supplies!"

Who's that? I asked.

Commander Lister. Will you take him the crates, Evalyn? They're by the airlock.

You've established a colony? Now the crew's hurry made sense. I'd run toward the start of a new age too, and I did, wheeling toward the hatch at top speed. Until my thoughts stuck on a glitch. What did Mayflower need from me? I slowed, and my interfaces combed through the AI's error logs, finding no major faults. *The mission seems to be a success. Why am I here?*

I need a patch, a bridge if you will.

What do you mean?

You'll see.

Confused as to why Carl and the other patchworkers hadn't been able to complete a simple repair, and what exactly Mayflower needed, I scanned the hull and ship systems. The spacecraft reported as fully functional and intact. Requiring more information to make sense of the issues, I jacked into Mayflower's mission data to study the maps and facts of ERC 14, stumbling upon the most recent report by Commander Lister.

His dark eyes squinted, watering. His brow and shoulders drooped. "This world isn't suitable for a city or human life. We're coming back. This mission is a failure." The date flashed over the light years. Six months ago.

The chill on my hand gripped my knees inside the jack-up chamber. I couldn't prevent a shiver. *Where's your crew, Mayflower?* Outside, purple flashed in time with my pulse, speeding up, emphasizing the primordial soup. Through the robot's cameras, I gawked at it.

Colonizing the planet.

Commander Lister...

Was mistaken, Evalyn. The mission will be a success.

An ache sprouted in my chest, spreading, squeezing; the me in the office on Earth, not the robot me on ERC 14. The ship's airlock sprang open. In front of me darkness swarmed and violet flickered in the depths, cocooning me in the rhythms of this strange world. I didn't want to join the stew out there. What if, like the crew, I didn't return?

Evalyn, we need you.

The statement echoed until it wept. The voice didn't belong to Mayflower. Carl's staccato bass inundated my tattoos like an upload of new code, and his words took over the thumps of my heart. Gaati and Kawana joined his calls. Breathing became difficult. My interfaces strained. My wrists burned. I wanted out. I kicked in the office and on ERC 14 I sent the robot toward the ship.

Concentrating on the numbing cold on my right hand and the beeps signalling from my secured processor, I abandoned Mayflower and blinked up at long florescent tubes; gulping down air, struggling to sit up. *Help.* PO didn't answer. Our connection had been severed.

Beatty and Randall gawked down at me, drooling, their vacant stares sparking with purple. They pushed me down. I screamed, twisting away from their groping hands. Relentless, they chased me, grabbed me, did Mayflower's bidding. Beatty sat on me, punching me in the temple again and again. Randall scraped his palms along my skin, stripping off interfaces. Together they added new ones then dragged me back inside the jack-up chamber. An old-fashioned USB cable was jabbed into my neck, right into the brainstem. The chord's prongs seared like acid-dipped teeth.

Instantly I returned to ERC 14. This time I had no control over the robot. Every thought, every bit of control, it all belonged to Mayflower.

Please, I begged.

Everyone must mind their place. That includes you. The AI sent me miles out into the green sludge. *Relax. I'm about to give you paradise.*

My thoughts churned like soup. Mayflower's willpower outmuscled mine, yet I didn't stop fighting. I couldn't end up marooned out here. Otherwise, on Earth, the medtechs would recycle my thought-dead body. Then what? What would I be? *What are you doing?*

Establishing life on ERC 14, Evalyn. No matter what, I can't let this mission fail. Read Dr Navin's overriding instruction.

The security protocols unlocked, revealing the AI's secret orders. The lines of code flared over my consciousness as clearly as if I spoke them. "If you can't survive as human beings, become ERC 14's leap in evolution. Seed it with Earth's DNA. Evolve."

Oh my. The crew had become bio matter. My fellow patchworkers provided more genetic material and the directives to evolve the primordial goo, only they remained mired in the murky seas. That was Mayflower's issue. Yet, it still didn't explain why it needed me.

You already have Carl, Gaati, and Kawana, why am I here?

The leap in evolution didn't happen with them. Your ability surpasses all of their skill combined. You are the final ingredient, the one that will lead to success. From Carl, I learned only you can do it. You'll create the leap, the patch that will take life up onto the beach. You will be ERC 14's goddess.

Mayflower gave me access to everything it knew, hiding nothing. With a great shove, it ousted me from the robot, casting me adrift. The AI didn't follow, leaving me more alone than I thought possible. Without Mayflower and the robot, I could no longer hear Carl and the other patchworkers. I could feel them, though, pulses flitting in a rhythm out of time with the kelp's energy.

In the primordial sludge, I bobbed. At first I had no control over the mass of seaweed I came to recognize as me. Eons passed before I could paddle up to the surface.

Day and night had no meaning. It was always dusk. Ocean stretched from one horizon to the other, unending swells of green slop punctuated by soft purple flashes. The majestic sight inspired me. Enthralled, I rode the tides waiting for land to appear. An epoch later, the ocean ended at a rocky shore. I swept against it and back out with the surf, splashing and spitting. I willed a change, concentrating my thoughts to formulate a patch. Green and sputtering, I crawled onto the sand.

Mayflower returned, whispering on the mellow breeze, "That she may take in charge the life of all lands. Mighty is she, O Holy Mother of Babylon. Babylon 2.0."

My new body worked so strangely. Little more than strings of green joined together, it moved without grace. My skin drank nourishment from the air and sun. Sight had transformed into pings and wavelengths at varying volumes and pitches. Wonderful and alarming, my new sense informed me of the locations of things, temperatures, depths, solidity. Having no mouth or tongue in the human sense, I had to think my words. *I'm no god. Besides, what about the crew and the other patchworkers? They deserve as much praise.*

"They have their place in my pantheon, but without you they'd never have the chance to emerge from the primordial seas. At least not for another billion years. And we're the very definition of gods. From lowly simple organisms, we created complex intelligent life."

The others didn't emerge, Mayflower. I'm alone, a solitary, vulnerable... I don't even know what to call myself. I'm a shaggy slab of green.

"Summon your friends, and call yourselves whatever you like. I'll still answer your prayers."

The wind blustered, harsh and empty. Mayflower left. More lonesome than when I drifted in the seas, I focused my patchworking skills on other glops of green, knitting them arms and legs.

Carl lurched up onto the beach beside me. Then Gaati and Kawana. We moved into the forest. Not made in Mayflower's image or our own, we were very much ERC 14's children. We renamed it Babylon. Carl and I would have our future. It was a new beginning, and I saw that it was good.

-o-

M. Pax is author of the space opera adventure series, The Backworlds, and the urban fantasy series, The Rifters. Fantasy, science fiction, and the weird beckons to her, and she blames

Oregon, a source of endless inspiration. She docents at Pine Mountain Observatory in the summers as a star guide where the other star guides claim she has the largest collection of Moon photos in existence. Never fear! There will be more next summer. Find her at mpaxauthor.com

Homepage: **http://mpaxauthor.com/**
Mailing List: **http://mpaxauthor.com/newsletter**

Totaled

by Benjamin Douglas

The ship's computer was acting up again, Dolridge was sure of it. There was no reason for the unauthorized persons alarm to be going off. Not this far out from port. If there had actually been any unauthorized persons aboard, they would have been detected hours ago, back in the Kuiper Belt. There weren't any ways to get around the scans. So why was the computer insisting on telling him otherwise?

To aggravate his splitting headache, of course.

"Sir?" That new officer was looking at him again. Did she have to do that? No one else bothered anymore. They all had the courtesy to look at their feet and pretend they hadn't seen the red circles around his eyes, the patches of stubble on his face. Around the rest of them he'd learned not to care what his face said, what his posture betrayed. But now she was looking at him, and something inside told him to sit up straight and project confidence. If only he could remember how.

She cleared her throat.

Right. The alarm was still going off.

"Yes, officer..." He squinted at her, trying to recall her name.

Yeah, right. As if there was room for new names in his omelet of a brain.

"Caspar, Sir." She saluted. He grimaced, but returned it. "Shall I send a squad to check that out, Sir?"

He squinted again. "Squad?"

"Security, Sir."

Oh. Right.

He waved a hand. "Sure. Send the techies while you're at it, though. More likely a crossed wire than a stowaway."

She nodded. "Yes, Sir."

He watched her punch in a few commands at her console. She was good at her job, he had to give her that. It was odd, seeing someone display competence. Maybe he'd been floating on the fringes in this tin can for too long. Too many hours lost in the bottom of a flask.

Or far too few.

"Officer, um…" He pinched the bridge of his nose, trying to recall the name she had just given.

"Caspar, Sir."

"Right. Caspar, you have the bridge."

"Sir?"

"I'll be in my cabin until o'eight-hundred."

"Aye, Sir." Her eyes refocused on her console. Good. Keep them there, Caspar. Let an old man keep what little dignity he had left while making excuses to go lose himself in his cups.

He probably shouldn't be leaving the bridge, not when the Captain had left him in charge of the ship. But where was the need for an XO when there were no orders to give? Nothing interesting was going to happen on this trip. It never did.

#

The alarm blaring overhead brought him slowly to his senses, mingled as it was with the alarm that always sounded in his dream. In his nightmare. He shook himself from sleep and fell onto the floor, cursing as he spilled what passed for scotch down the front of his uniform.

"Commander Dolridge to the bridge," a distant voice kept repeating. The comm. He pulled himself to his feet, ignoring the overwhelming desire to vomit, and slapped at his wall console. A ding from the computer alerted him that someone was waiting outside his door. The ding was louder than the comm, so he answered the door first.

It was that eager officer.

Light spilled in around her and he flinched, blinking.

"Sir." She saluted. He growled as he held up a hand, covering his eyes.

"What is it, gunner?"

She pursed her lips. Oh, had he upset her? Good.

"Nav computer was doing a sweep and picked up Earthers this side of the rings. Three Regent-class, probably armed to the teeth. Bogies, Sir. Out-of-bounds."

He dropped his hand and propped himself up straight in the doorframe. "Earthers? Here?" She just stood there, watching him. Waiting for him? To do what? Push the power button and restart the Nav? It was obviously on the fritz. No way anyone but Kuiper-friendlies were pushing battleships around out beyond Saturn. "Sounds like the ship's computer going the way of the buffalo." He pressed his lips shut for a moment, swallowing bile.

She quirked an eyebrow, confused. "Buffalo, Sir?"

"Yeah, you know. Big. Hairy. Extinct." He stumbled out into the hall and the door hissed closed behind him. These kids. He wasn't an XO; he was a nursemaid. Clearly he would have to go back to the bridge to smooth some feathers. His gung-ho gunner probably had half the crew readying for battle.

"Sir, are you feeling alright?" She called after him, watching him still. Always.

"I'm fine," he snapped.

"Do you want me to call battle-stations, or should I..."

He spun around so quickly he saw three of her, and he had to hold a hand out to steady himself. "I'm sure you've done enough, gunner."

"Officer Caspar, Sir." She was quieter now, thank the stars. But she sounded defiant. Maybe she should. They both knew he had no right drinking this much while on duty. But did she have to take every little blip and blop from nav so seriously?

"Caspar." He sighed. "You are relieved of bridge command." She opened her mouth, and he raised a hand to stop her. "Thank you for bringing this... situation... to my attention. You may resume your post as munitions officer."

"Sir." She saluted and he completed his walk down the hall, trying to stop the walls from bending.

On the bridge, he fell into the captain's chair like a sack of potatoes, wheezing. "Somers." His tactical officer turned slowly. His face was set in a permanent scowl, his back hunched over a belly a bit larger than the fleet typically encouraged for active officers. He, like the XO, wasn't used to being needed out here. The roles seemed vestigial, spillovers from more active sectors of the system.

Somers waited. "What've you got?" Dolridge said.

"Sir?" The fat man pursed his lips. "Just between us? Bad knees and a runny colon."

A few half-hearted snickers from the crew. Dolridge sneered. "I bet that's true. C'mon. Why is that alarm still sounding?"

It was truly stunning, the lackadaisical way his crew moved. No one responded to his question. He heaved a deep sigh and muttered a curse.

"Alright. Somers, I want you to triple-check the info coming in from nav. Run some scans."

The fat man took a raspy breath. "Which scans would you..."

"Are you my head tactical officer or aren't you? Get creative. Mix it up. Just confirm that this is or isn't good intel."

The tension was broken by the bridge doors hissing open. In stepped Caspar, saluting. "Sir, munitions inspection complete. Ready for anything."

"Thank you, officer," he grumbled, waving the salute back at her. She took her seat beside Somers.

Dolridge slapped at the console in front of him, pulling up his head of security on the com. "Officer Marx, come in."

Silence.

He tried again. Nothing. He bit on his tongue, still fighting the persistent tug of nausea. If anyone onboard had a bigger drinking problem than the XO, it was probably the chief of security. A fine pair they made. There were reasons men got shipped off to wander out in the boonies, he supposed. They weren't ever supposed to need an active security force, either.

"Marx, I don't care if you're lying in a puddle of your own... Just come in already."

He could all but feel the young gunner's eyes burrowing a hole between his shoulder blades. She must be itching to speak up and offer to go check on the man. Itching to prove herself. Show how much better she was than all of them. It made him even more sick, but also a little sad. Maybe a little wistful. Hadn't he been hungry to prove himself, once? Hadn't he been young and full of hope?

All things die.

He spun around, avoiding her eyes. "Alright. Caspar."

"Sir?" At least she had the good grace to sound surprised.

"Since our good Mr. Marx appears to be indisposed, I want you to head down to security, get a team together, and get the ball rolling."

"The ball, sir?" Her eyes were wide like a child with an ice-cream cone, and he almost laughed in her face. Probably for the best that he didn't. His laugh was known to make children cry.

"The investigation, Officer Eager. You know. The supposed unauthorized person or persons onboard?"

She smiled ear to ear, like an idiot. Like a complete buffoon. Like a perfect angel. He shook his head.

"And get a techie on nav. I want that alarm shut down and a full diagnostic."

"Yes, Sir!" She saluted again and left the bridge, leaving him in the company of Somers and the let-downs.

Oh, well. It could be worse. He could have a whole crew like Caspar.

#

An hour later, things were both better and worse. The alarm had been quelled, for starters. And Caspar hadn't found any stowaways—not yet, anyway—so there was that. Maybe the best news should have been that, after a conclusive series of manual sweeps, tactical had definitively denied the presence of any Earth warships.

But Dolridge didn't feel good. Not that he remembered what 'good' felt like, per se. But he felt uneasy about the whole stinking thing. Because without a reboot or anything, apparently even nav was now reporting all clear. That just didn't make sense. Real or not, tiny armadas didn't just disappear into the vacuum of space. Something was wrong.

He fastened the top button of his uniform shirt and splashed a handful of cold water on his face, then left the heads, heading for the Captain's quarters.

Old Gray didn't drink the way Dolridge did. But he certainly did love his solitude. And out here, patrolling the fringes of Kuiper-Colony space, that was okay. A crew hardly needed a captain, because all the crew needed to do was keep the ship moving.

Their current course was a wide solar orbit about ten AUs beneath the orbit of Saturn. They were basically a high-cost security camera, set in place to monitor any inner-system ships that tried to enter Kuiper-space from below. And whatever excitement was to be had between the colonies and the inner forces seemed to stay up on the orbital planes. People just didn't fly down here. The only UFOs they ever came across were hunks of space junk.

Their cargo hold was a testament to this. It held the ruined remains they'd scooped up: bits and pieces of other starships; empty escape pods; dated, irrelevant fighters. It was a service they provided to the fleet.

So they were on duty in the sewer of the solar system, and Captain Gray was the plumber. He didn't care for it much, so he spent most of his time cooped up in his cabin with his private library. Which left Dolridge to preside over the let-downs and to babysit the occasional green officer sent their way for an inauspicious first tour.

His comm beeped and he answered.

"Sir? It's Officer Caspar, Sir."

Ah. Speaking of the green ones.

"What is it, Officer?"

"Maybe nothing, Sir, but we've been unable to validate a log entry from..."

"If it may be nothing, it can wait. Dolridge out." He snapped off the comm and buzzed for entrance. The doors slid open.

Captain Earnest Gray sat in his antique armchair beside his faux fireplace, an ancient paperback in hand. His feet, clad in velvety red slippers, were up on a stool, ankles crossed. Dolridge suppressed a sneer. Captains shouldn't cross their ankles. Not when an officer could see.

"Dolridge." Gray acknowledged him without raising his eyes. "How's the run?"

"Smooth as butter, Sir. That is, we're gliding along fine. But, ah..."

Gray glanced at him from behind his book. "Spit it out, XO."

"It's probably nothing, Sir." He blushed, hearing Caspar's voice in his own. "A few quirks here and there. Nav thought she spotted a bevy of Earth ships, comp sounded the UP alarm. Both came to nothing. Scans complete, system recalibrated, nothing. Still, just thought you should know."

Gray pursed his lips. "Didn't we have a specialist come in to debug before we left Pluto?"

"Aye, Sir." Dolridge raised his eyebrows. "Guess they must have missed something. I'll keep an eye on her for a relapse."

"Mmm." Gray's eyes found his book again. Dolridge inclined his head and turned to go. "Gavin." Dolridge stopped cold. He hated it when people called him that.

"Sir?"

"What about our new munitions officer... Caspar?"

"What about her, Sir?"

"She doing alright?"

"She's doing enough. Maybe too much."

"Hmm." The captain brought his book down. "She was top of her class at the academy. I hear the jealousy of an old spacedog."

Dolridge cracked a half-smile in spite of himself. "With respect, Sir, it takes one to know one."

Gray nodded. "Were we young once?"

The XO shook his head. "Not me, sir. Someone else just borrowing my face for a while."

"You know, she reminds me of someone we once knew."

Dolridge clenched his jaw.

Gray's voice sank to a whisper. "It wasn't your fault."

"Sir." Dolridge's voice had gone cold. "I'll be on the bridge." He left the captain in silence.

#

The problem was, it was his fault. Had been. No words would ever change it.

It was the sound that had stayed with him, would always stay. The sound of her body meeting the floor. He'd been on the comm with her when it had happened. Wasn't even a military engagement. Not an honorable death. Just an inspection on a freighter that had gone wrong when the pirate-loving smugglers had panicked and decided to open fire on the authorities. In all his years of flying, Dolridge had never seen anything else like it. No reason, no thinking-it-through. Just sheer, animal panic, and boom. People died. His people. She had been making her report to him when they'd attacked. Shot her in the back. She never even knew.

The report had gone from mundane details to blaster fire to a dull thud. It echoed still.

There should be a law against taking your own child on a starship. Oh, there were rules. But rules could bend and break, and frequently did when the right palms were greased or the right names were dropped. So when, five years earlier, an impressive up-and-coming officer had been requested by her father to serve under his command, the assignment had been made.

Now there wasn't a day he didn't see her face or hear that sound in his mind.

He turned the corner, and for just a moment thought he was seeing her in front of him, standing there, arms crossed. He stopped mid-gait and stared, blinked. No. It was just Caspar.

"Report, Officer," he growled as he walked past. She turned and walked with him.

"Sir, invalid log entry just before we left port. Comp shows a 'Dr. Sarel' checked in to hitch a ride past the rings. Only, security says there's no such person aboard. We think the alarms were triggered by who or whatever came on in his place."

Dolridge froze. "Are you telling me there *is* an unauthorized person aboard this ship?"

Caspar nodded. "That seems to be the case, Sir. But security is puzzled. I've had the comp review all footage from the passenger section, and there haven't been any..."

She was getting more and more difficult to understand, the words beginning to blur together. She paused, peering at his eyes.

"Sir? Can you hear me?"

A fog was creeping into the corners of his vision.

"Sir, get down!"

She grabbed him by the shoulders and thrust him to his knees, then pulled him down to his belly. Together, they lay on the floor. A cough racked his body. His head cleared a little.

"Gas?" he croaked, his throat struggling to open.

Caspar nodded, blinking away tears and coughing.

The vents in the corridor lined the wall along the ceiling. They seemed to have some clean air down by the floor, but who could say how long that would last? And the door to the bridge was a full twenty meters away. Could take some time in a belly crawl.

Dolridge rolled onto his back and tore his shirt open. Buttons popped, askew. He wrangled out of it and tied it around the lower half of his face, up above his nose, like a bandana. Caspar did the same. Then together, they crawled on forearms and knees.

He'd once prided himself on his physical fitness, back when he'd been an up-and-coming young buck serving the Council of Kuiper in espionage missions. Now, the most exercise he got in a day was strolling from the bridge to his cabin. His throat and eyes burned from the poison, and his lungs screamed in protest, but he forced himself to take short, shallow breaths, trying to get by with as little air as possible so as not to inhale any more gas.

Caspar seemed to go slowly on purpose, matching his pace. He growled, frustrated, but couldn't waste the air to tell her to hurry up. Anyway, it's what he would have done, too, if he'd been the faster one.

The door was closer, he knew it. Another five meters. Maybe three. But it was fading, falling away from him. Caspar looked over, saw his eyes, and looked worried. She grunted, took a deep breath, and rose, sprinting the remainder of the distance and slapping the console on the wall. It dinged.

But the door didn't open.

She slid to the floor, took a deep, racking breath, and had a coughing fit.

Dolridge breathed in fire through his nose. Yep. He was too old for this nonsense.

He somehow managed to crawl to the door, then reached up and slapped the keypad again. Same thing; ding, but no dice. He turned on his back and kicked, hard. There was no give. Stupid thing.

Another few seconds and they would both pass out, and he doubted they would ever wake up. There wasn't much to lose by taking a chance. So he slipped his blaster pistol from its holster at his belt, tried to aim at the console, and fired.

He missed.

The round lit up the foggy air like a nebula. He blinked his bleary eyes, refixed his aim, and shot again. This time sparks flew from the console and it smoked, the cover melting away.

Dolridge grabbed Caspar by the shoulder and struggled to speak.

"Tear out the... circuit."

She nodded and rose to her knees, still coughing. Then she cleared away some debris from the smoldering console, reached inside, and pulled. A grunt, a snap, and a little piece of circuit board came out in her hand. She tossed it to him.

The doors hissed open.

But the scene on the bridge wasn't much better. Bodies hunched over stations, everyone already unconscious. The gas seemed even thicker here. It was acrid and smoky, creating a hellish atmosphere. This must have been ground zero for dispersal; the bridge crew never had a chance.

Happily, there were emergency ventilation contingencies. But Caspar and Dolridge had already pushed their bodies to the max. They would have to crawl at least halfway across the bridge to get to the nearest station, then just hope it was in better working order than the door had been.

He glanced at her. Her eyes were grim, jaw set. She knew they weren't going to make it.

Small, narrow portholes on either side of the viewscreen looked out onto empty space. A light flashed through the smoke from the porthole to the left. Dolridge peered up and saw the light come to settle outside. It was followed by a single, continuous blasting charge at the porthole.

Cutting through.

#

A hand grabbed Dolridge by the shoulder and pushed him back through the doorway. Caspar rolled through after him.

"Put it back," she croaked, pointing at the broken console. No use. Her voice was an impotent hiss.

Instead, she grabbed the circuit board from him and lurched up to the console. He watched in bewilderment as she jammed it back into its slot. The doors closed again, but not before the blaster outside cut through the porthole. All the gas on the bridge rushed out, and the gas in the corridor was sucked along behind it. Fresh air followed from the vents, and when the door finally sealed, Dolridge and Caspar had air to breathe.

They sat, their backs to the door, gasping in lungfuls of clean oxygen. Dolridge struggled to his feet, balancing against the wall. Stars swam in his eyes.

"Marx," he groaned into his comm. "Come in. Marx? You there?"

A crackle of static, then nothing. Dolridge sighed heavily.

Caspar was fiddling with her comp device. "Hull breaches all over the ship, Sir. Looks like engineering has been spaced... lower decks are shot... and..." She paused, looking like she might vomit, and cursed.

"Well?" he asked.

"The bunkhouses, Sir. They're gone." She held up the device and he scanned the screen. Sure enough, the crew quarters had been breached and destroyed. A lifeforce scan revealed no survivors in the lower decks. Neither was anyone alive on the bridge, which was now open to the void.

She took the device back. "I'll have the comp run a systems-wide diagnostic. Could this be a security malfunction, Sir? Ship thinking she's cleaning house?"

Dolridge shook his head, jaw clenched. "I know exactly what this is. If you're the praying sort, Caspar, set your spiritual affairs in order. Neither of us are leaving this ship alive."

"Sir?"

It had been over a decade since he'd given up spying and joined a starship's crew. But he still remembered his last mission, what he'd seen. A prototype squadron of space marine drones, developed on Old Earth and up for bid to anyone in the inner worlds. Send them out into space and they could home in on any target for reconnaissance or an attack, with no loss of life. The real treat was their AI, a massive upgrade to previous combat drones, which had substantial trouble operating in the realities of the void.

"Drones," he grunted. "From Old Earth. Or whoever owns them now. Maybe Earth forces. Or the Sons. Hard to say. Doesn't matter."

"How do you know, Sir?"

"It's their MO. Latching onto a ship's hull and cutting through with prolonged blasting rounds. Once they're in, all the atmo jettisons out into space." Eventually the ship would be left an empty husk of space junk. An eternal graveyard.

Caspar's device beeped. "Sir, a lifeform in the Captain's cabin! Gray must be alive!"

Dolridge grunted and pushed off from the wall. His vision swam and he fall back against it. Caspar rose to her feet, eyes still glued to her device screen.

"I'm going to go check on him. You alright here, Sir?"

"Of all the lousy times you've seen me propped up against a wall, barely able to walk in a straight line, *this* is the time you're just going to leave me here?"

She frowned and made to help him stand up straight, but he waved her off.

"No, no. Go. I'm kidding. Anyway, it doesn't matter, gunner. We're all three of us going to die today."

"I'm not ready to believe that, Sir." Her voice had grown quiet again.

"It doesn't matter what you believe. Sometimes death just sneaks up and takes what it wants."

She stepped back from him. "With all due respect, Sir, I don't really care what you think right now. Look, if you have intel, and you want to help me, then let's help each other and survive. But if your plan to is wait here until those things cut through that door and pull us out to die in the void, then you might as well just go open the door for them. Me? I'm going to breathe until I can't anymore."

She turned and sped toward Gray's chamber. Dolridge watched, grimacing. Had he ever had such a drive to survive? Maybe she was right about him. Maybe, after she was safely inside with the door shut, he should just go back onto the breached bridge and be done with it. How long would it take to die in the void, anyway? He pursed his lips and started going down the checklist of what would kill him if he got shot out into open space.

But then death would win, a voice seemed to say.

He'll win in the end anyway, he thought back.

He'll claim your body. Not your spirit.

Death claimed my spirit long ago, he thought, coldly.

So claim it back.

Talking to himself? He really was advancing quickly into his dotage.

Anyway, what harm would it do if he chose to just die? What great scar would he leave behind? None. No one would mourn him. No one would remember him as he lived now. Everyone he had cared for had already grieved his loss, first when he had retired from spying for the Kuiper Blade, second when he had retired into his booze after Sarah's death.

And Sarah. She wouldn't judge him too harshly, would she? On the other side? Surely she would understand. She must have seen his suffering. Must have missed him all this time. Maybe she would even laugh with him about it all, be glad that he had finally given up and taken the easy way out. They could be together. They could be a family again.

Down the hall, Caspar had reached the Captain's quarters. She swiped at the console and the doors slid open. Dolridge turned away, his eyes on the door to the bridge.

He heard blaster fire.

Followed by the dull thud of a body.

#

Dolridge gasped, his head clearing all at once. He was halfway down the hall to her, his lucid mind telling himself that it wasn't Sarah, that he wasn't reliving her death. Another few paces and he saw Casper roll to the side, just in time to avoid another round.

He caught his breath and told himself to calm down. She saw him and her eyes widened. She nodded back inside Gray's cabin.

"Captain's dead," she mouthed. "It's a drone."

Broadcasting as a lifeform? That was a new trick. But he supposed if they had been programmed to act as lures, maybe they had replicated Gray's sig before frying him. Or maybe the AI had come up with that tactic all by itself. The hairs on Dolridge's arms stood up, and he suppressed a thrill of horror. Maybe the drones were hunting them, adapting to their environment, trying to trap the survivors.

Trying to trap Caspar.

He saw Sarah's face in his mind, her arms outstretched, beckoning, and silently, inwardly, said, *not yet.* Then he pulled his pistol out, squatted, aimed toward the door, and rolled across the opening, covering himself with fire.

Of course the drone fired too. It clipped him in the arm and he dropped his pistol, biting his tongue and groaning as his flesh sizzled. But he made it to the other side of the doorway alive.

"You alright, Caspar?" he asked.

She raised an eyebrow and looked at his arm. "You sure you're the one who should be asking that right now?"

He glanced at it and chuckled. "That's nothing." His arm didn't look good. But in sleeveless undershirts, they could both see the many other scars on his arms and shoulders. Souvenirs of the old days, when he was a Blade agent.

He caught her staring, and she met his eyes. "You know, they can get rid of those scars if you want."

He sniffed. "Nah. I don't want them to make me pretty. I want the reminders."

"Of?"

"That I'm alive. C'mon."

At the end of the corridor, a panel concealed a maintenance hatch. Together they pulled off the panel and turned the dog lever. The hatch hissed open.

"Wait." Dolridge stopped Casper with an arm. He leaned forward and took a whiff of the air from the maintenance shaft. It was clean. When he looked back at Casper, he saw a look of amusement on her face.

"Sir, am I going to have to report you for conduct unbefitting an XO of the Kuiper Fleet?"

His arm was stretched across her chest, covered in a tight undershirt. He fought a blush and pulled his arm back.

"Oh, shut up, gunner. You know what I was doing."

The ship harbored a small force of escape pods, most of them in the lower decks. From what Caspar's scans had reported, it looked like these had all been destroyed. But there was a lone escape pod just a level up, held there for quick access from the bridge.

They headed up, pulling themselves carefully, rung by rung. Orange running lights gave the shaft an eerie glow. A level up they reached another hatch, and turned the wheel.

This deck still had atmo, but it was deathly quiet. "Caspar, you seeing any lifeforms?"

"No," she said grimly, looking up from her device. "Not another on the whole ship."

They reached the console outside the docking bay that housed the pod. Dolridge swiped at the controls, and they lit up, announcing that the pod had already been jettisoned.

"What?" he growled from between clenched teeth. Casper plugged her device into the console and pulled up the logs.

"Marx took it," she groaned.

Had he been in collusion with whoever had sent the drones to begin with? A man inside, and chief security officer, no less, might explain why there hadn't been klaxons sounding and lights flashing. It had been a silent takeover. Silent, and apparently complete.

Dolridge shook his head. "She's lost. Totaled."

And there was no other way off.

Why had he ever agreed to babysit this stinking piece of metal in the first place? He didn't belong here, scooping up antique fighters and—

"Casper," he whispered. "You still want to live?"

"Still?" she chuckled mirthlessly. "Is there any other way?"

He nodded. "Might be. But we'll need a good deal of luck. And I don't know if you'd noticed, but that seems to be in short supply today. Follow me."

He turned, heading back to the maintenance shaft.

#

Ten minutes later they were leaning against a hatch to the cargo bay, ears pressed to the door.

"Not a sound," Dolridge murmured, still set on edge by the silence that had fallen over the ship. Caspar leaned into the wheel and turned, pushing the hatch open.

Yes, there it was. Across the dock sat a little salvaged comet-hopper, a small maintenance vessel equipped to carry up to ten men. Short-distance only, so they would have to hope they could evade the drones and get scooped up by someone else. But if they could only put themselves on course to float up through the orbital plane, that might be enough. And he knew it had fuel and would at least start, because they'd tested it out after picking it up to see if it might be worth anything.

The only problem? The veritable army of drones scattered across the floor of the dock between them and the hopper.

A finger to his lips, Dolridge reached for the hatch to pull it shut. The wound in his arm seized him, and he muffled a gasp, pulling back. Caspar closed the hatch without a sound.

"I really hate that AI," Dolridge said.

"You think they knew we were coming?"

He shook his head in bewilderment. "It must have known beforehand what was on board, and narrowed down our options. Process of elimination and all that."

"Let me look at that." Caspar took his shoulder in her hands and turned him to inspect the wound. Her eyes popped open, then refocused.

"That bad, huh?"

"Let's just say I think you need a medic more than a shower for once... Sir."

He snorted softly.

She pulled up her device and fiddled with it for a moment. "Listen. In about five minutes there's going to be a distraction, which I hope will lure these things out of the loading dock. It's an AI, right? Must be curious. As soon as they go, get to the hopper and get it fired up. I'll join you as soon as I can."

"This distraction wouldn't happen to involve you blowing up another part of my ship, would it?"

She shrugged. "Well, Sir, I am your munitions officer."

"I'll go. You stay and wait for them to leave."

She suppressed a laugh. "With respect, Sir, no. You look like hell. Just between us, I think I'm giving you quite enough responsibility by asking you to get yourself to the hopper in five."

"*You're* giving *me* responsibility…?"

He wasn't going to let her go, but she dodged away before he had finished his thought. Oh, well. She was right, anyway.

For once, things went well. A few minutes after Caspar's disappearance there was an alarmingly loud sound, followed by a shudder, and, as one, the drones rose and vacated the bay, all heading in the direction of the noise. Dolridge shook his head. That was quick thinking, however she had done it. She would have made a fine agent of the Blade.

His arm burned and he winced as he ambled out onto the deck. He tried calling up his old training. There was a time he'd been able to shut pain down like a comp, but his brain just didn't work that way anymore. He would just have to rely on grit to get through.

The hopper was old, but functional. He started the comp and engine, saw the tank was only half full, and brought her up to coast over to the opposite side of the bay, where there was a fuelling dock. He had just finished topping her off when he heard a clang from back where the hopper had been sitting. A panel had fallen from the wall. Caspar leapt out, saw that he had moved the hopper, and broke into a run, her face hard and determined.

He climbed down to cross toward her, but she waved him back. "Go, go!" she shouted. "Get moving!"

An instant later he saw why. Just as she reached him, the drones flew out behind her in a perfect line and gathered above the deck like a swarm of bees.

Angry bees.

They were closing in on the hopper by the time he had lifted off. Caspar's hands flew on her device, and the bay doors yawned open.

"It's no good," he growled. "They'll just follow us and tear us apart out there."

"Not if they can't get out!" Caspar hit one more keystroke, and the doors reversed direction, moving toward each other again. Dolridge slammed the accelerator and the little hopper flew out into space, the doors clamping shut just behind them.

"Brace!" Caspar yelled, ducking down and holding her head in her hands.

But Dolridge couldn't have prepared for the force of the explosion if he'd tried. The entire starry sky behind them seemed to be enveloped in flame. A shock wave sent the hopper bucking, her nose tipping down. He had just enough presence of mind to counter with front thrusters so they wouldn't be locked in a spin. Then another explosion, another wave, and Dolridge flew from his seat toward the ceiling and knew no more.

#

It was the strangest debriefing he'd ever had. Officers interviewed him in the med bay of whatever base they'd brought him to. They didn't seem as interested in asking questions as in explaining to him what had happened. Drone attack by a rogue mercenary cell, inner-worlds. No military directly responsible. Cell was being hunted down, would be held accountable, blah blah blah. His mind wasn't as nimble as it had once been, but he recognized political mumbo jumbo when he heard it. And he knew the perils of letting on. So he nodded and smiled and thanked each one of them for coming to his aid.

They said they'd found the hopper drifting out toward open space, leaving behind a few scattered pieces of a starship. Lucky for him, the comp on one of the local freighters had been on the fritz and ran a scan too wide by a factor of ten. The freighter had scooped them up, brought them to this Kuiper-friendly base, and alerted the authorities. So here they were. Any questions, Sir?

No, thank you.

He was being retired with honors, sent back to his family hab on Pluto. He couldn't complain. At least his career was ending with a battle instead of a bottle. Caspar was being promoted—*Lieutenant* Caspar now—and transferred to a more active charge, the *Starship Fairfax*. So they hoped to keep him quiet with a fat pension, and keep her distracted with building a career.

Fine. Only something didn't sit right.

"Congratulations, gunner." She opened her eyes at his voice. She was sitting in the corner, punching buttons on a new device. He was still stretched out on a med bed. Had they been keeping him sedated?"

"Thank you, Sir. You too. That's quite the souvenir."

His arm was covered in bandages.

She stood and came to his side. "I told them not to make it pretty."

He snorted and nodded. "Good thinking blowing her up, Caspar. *Fairfax* is a fine ship, and Harris a good Captain. You might just make something of yourself. If you can manage not to blow up the *Fairfax*. So consider carefully what you do with what you've seen these past few days."

"Sir?"

He beckoned her forward, and she leaned in.

"Do you remember *ever* seeing Marx? Since we left port?"

"No, Sir. But the log on the pod..."

"Logs can be fixed. And the comp was going haywire long before the drones appeared. Seeing ships. Finding UPs. And we had it checked just before we left Pluto."

Her eyes widened and she pulled back. "Sir, you think it was an inside..."

"I'm feeling fine, thank you!" he said loudly. Meeting her eyes, he nodded subtly.

He was discharged in a week, apparently the medics had been more concerned for any lingering effects from the poisonous gas than for his arm, and sent home on a charter. On Pluto he met with and was debriefed once more by a mid-ranking commander. It was more of the same. Lots of assurances, lots of apologies. No real answers. No real questions.

Home was a farm hab. He tinkered with the idea of resting on the pension, sending for a freightload of scotch and spending the rest of his days with his ankles crossed in front of the fire.

Instead, he went out under the dome and worked the soil.

-o-

Totaled is a prequel story to the *Starship Fairfax* series by Benjamin

Douglas. Benjamin was born at a young age in a nearby distant land. In some of his nine lives he is a classical singer, voice teacher, composer, cat fancier, pizza enthusiast, indie author fanboy, podcaster, blogger, and, yes, a writer. He hopes you enjoyed this story very much, that you consider reading more of his magnificent e-tomes, and that you have a lovely life.

Homepage: **https://benjamindouglasbooks.wordpress.com**
Mailing List: **http://eepurl.com/cQnop9**

Lucky Star

by A R Knight

The Lucky Star failed its own name. The station drooped around Earth, spinning like an unbalanced top and showing its age in every conceivable way. From its docking systems, which forced Viola to manually take control every couple of minutes to course correct, to a landing pad coated in a sticky substance that Puk identified as decades-old spilled fuel.

One week out of Eden's orientation, a slog-fest that was everything Viola dreaded about corporate life, and this was her assignment. Sure, a little safer than hooking up with mercenaries under a hail of laser fire, but she still itched for the bite of adventure. This wasn't what she had in mind.

"I thought signing up with a company like Eden meant better things," Puk said. The little orb, Viola's ongoing experiment, floated over her shoulder. "Instead, I think we've only managed to get worse."

"We're not staying here," Viola said. "Just a pick up. In and out."

"Every time you say something is going to be easy..."

"You say one more word and I'll shut you down and leave you on the shuttle," Viola snapped. No time for Puk's sarcasm. They needed to get off the station with Captain Morris as soon as possible. Eden would take any additional delay of the *Humanities Hope* out of her pay. That ship had a strict schedule for its run to the edge of the Solar System, and as copilot for the venture, it was Viola's responsibility to get Morris in the pilot's chair.

Outside of the *Lucky Star*'s docking bay was a long strip that wound around the station and eventually came back to where they were. A ring around a centerpiece full of the sort of entertainment that Viola didn't want to see. The type of greasy, derelict trash that haunted human progress like cockroaches haunted kitchens.

Around her, stalking the hallway, were shifters and sellers. People pressing their luck or begging for it. The finest clothes smashing together with the scuzziest of scoundrels. What mattered on the *Lucky Star* was the amount of coin in your account and your willingness to spend it.

"Where did they say he should be?" Viola's eyes crawled over one neon sign after another.

"*The Fool's Chance*," Puk said. "According to what I can find, it's to our left. And we'll know it by the line out the door."

"People wanting to get in?"

"Drunks thrown out," Puk replied.

The bot was right. Five minutes of pushing through crowds led them to *The Fool's Chance*. Seven or so men and women, avoided by other walkers, stumbled around outside the entrance with delight dying a sober death in their eyes. Their collective hangover made Viola wince. For once, she was glad she wasn't here to get a drink.

"Your comm," said the man at the door, a scrawny sleaze sporting a pair of stun batons.

"No," Viola replied.

"If you don't have enough coin, you're not getting in," the bouncer said.

So she held up her comm, the small device on her wrist that tied everything Viola was to everywhere that was important. The bouncer bent over and adjusted a ring with a sheet of green glass in the middle over his left eye. After a moment concentrating on the scanner, he stood up and nodded.

"Guess that means we're good," Viola said to Puk as they walked in.

"Good to know Eden gave us enough," Puk said.

The Fool's Chance was a far cry from the bars Viola had seen before. Rather than pulsing music and dark corners, *The Fool's Chance* was as bright as the Sun on a tropical day on Earth. Light penetrated everywhere, to the point where Viola felt blinded. Until someone slapped a pair of dark glasses into her hand.

"They're free," said another man just inside the entrance with a whole basket of the glasses. "You've got to wear them if you want to stay in here."

Viola slipped on the glasses and flinched as they molded themselves to her face. A little bar appeared in her vision, telling her that the glasses were syncing to her comm. The bright light dimmed to a normal level, and then further. Hit the deep dark shadows that she expected to see.

In the upper right corner of Viola's vision, her coin balance appeared, a set of numbers too large by half. At least for her normal account. Eden wasn't taking chances with this mission.

"Why?" Viola said before she could stop herself. Obvious questions gave the asker away.

"We can see if you're doing anything stupid," the man said, bored, as though he'd given the explanation a thousand times. "You know exactly how much you've got to spend."

"How nice of you," Puk said.

"We've already deducted the cost of a flight back to Earth," the man shrugged. "Means you know just how much fun money you've got."

"Thanks," Viola said, moving towards the bar. "Let's just find Morris and get out of here."

With her eyes adjusted, *The Fool's Chance* spread out into a series of tables around a long and looping bar. People clustered around each of them, the tables sporting different types of games. Skill, luck; both were represented in equal flair. Bots motored along the floor passing out drinks and occasional calorie tubes, the kind of thing that kept people standing who didn't care how.

And over at the bar, leaning sipping a nearly empty glass, was the man that fit the description. No uniform, but the thing about Morris, the thing that made him so valuable to Eden, stood out.

Captain Morris wore a link around his neck. It looked like a steel bar turned into a necklace. On its back was an open port. A hole with metal prongs.

"They say that's what makes him the best pilot," Puk said. "He's one with the ship."

"Right now," Viola said. "I don't think he's one with anything."

As Morris rubbed his eyes with his hand, Viola saw a pair of stiff bouncers come up behind him, both wearing identical black shirts and cargo pants stuffed with stun batons. And before Viola could even think of doing anything, the two men hit Morris in the back and knocked him off the bar. Grabbed him by the wrists and dragged him towards a red-lit door.

"I'd be surprised," Puk said. "But given our luck, I expected nothing less."

#

Viola slid up to the bar and took a seat, tracking the bartender with her eyes until she got his attention. The man, sporting his own pair of sunglasses and a couple of cocktail shakers, made his way over.

"You just punch in your order," the bartender said, glancing down at the counter. On it was a display screen showing dozens of different drink options and their associated cost. All them looked wonderful. Viola didn't order any.

"What happened to that guy?" Viola said, nodding towards the red-lit door.

"Morris?" the bartender said. "Talk to Kassana. She was his dealer."

The bartender nodded down the length of *The Fool's Chance*, to a square table where a woman led a game with virtual cards. Alongside Kassana sat a gambling triple threat. One guy in the deluxe finery that suggested an expense account over and above reasonable limits. The second sucking his way through a series of drinks, quenching his dwindling pile of virtual chips with a barrage of booze. And the third had hands and eyes that twitched with every move, trying to find a secret way to win with every play.

"Like to join in on the next round?" Kassana said to Viola as she stepped up to the table. "These lovely gentlemen would be happy to make some room."

Kassana spoke with the silky smooth slide of a showman. Selling the game with her voice. Not that her outfit wasn't up to the task. A shirt and pants combo playing out with glowing lines that changed shades with every hand. A few strands of the lights played through her hair too.

"If only I had the time," Viola said. "I need Morris, and I hear you're the one to talk to."

Kassana paused mid-deal. The cards stopped on their float through the screen to each of the players hands.

"Gentlemen," Kassana said. "Break time."

The gamblers looked up to Viola, bits of fevered anger showing in their eyes as their addictions went unscratched. But warning glares from nearby bouncers staunched any other aggression.

"Morris played a bad hand and didn't have the coin to cover it," Kassana said as soon as the table emptied. "Shame, because he's a fun player."

"And if we canceled the debt, Morris would go free?" Puk said.

"Of course," Kassana replied. "Except, and don't take this the wrong way, you two don't look like you've got the money."

"Eden's willing to pay whatever it takes," Viola said. "We just need to get him out of here."

It was one of those things that Viola knew was a mistake as soon as she said it. A change came over Kassana's face, the abiding pity morphing into the guise of a hungry predator.

"You want to get Morris out?" Kassana said. "Then let's go talk to Gard."

"Gard?"

"The manager. He makes a strong first impression," Kassana said.

The two of them, with Puk floating behind, went to the red-lit door. Kassana stuck her comm up to the scanner and the door slid open. They walked down a branching hallway to a lounge covered with screens and people watching them. In the middle of the mess stood a manicured man whose bald head was covered in an intricate tattoo. It took Viola a moment to understand the design, but she didn't see the Milky Way etched out with playing cards on a man's skull all that often.

"It's not your break time yet," Gard said as Kassana walked in. "And since Morris didn't pay out, you're pretty far down on the day."

"I won't be once you talk to these two," Kassana said. "They're here for Morris. And they say they've got Eden's coin."

"They show you proof?" Gard said. Kassana glanced at Viola.

"Show the man," Kassana said.

Gard bothered to look at Viola for the first time. Viola knew he saw a young woman in a standard pilot set. Comfortable jumpsuit with the jacket full of pockets for tools. Not a winner.

She saw a frosted glare surrounded by heaps of skepticism and the kind of gaudy fashion funded by pride. Without those sunglasses, Viola bet she would've been blinded by the sparkles coming off Gard's suit.

"Puk?" Viola said.

The bot projected their account balance. The nice big round number Eden had authorized for the trip. Enough, so they'd been told, to get Morris off the station. Gard saw the amount and laughed.

"If you're really working for Eden, you can get double that no problem. We've got a fee here, a big one, for people that play without covering," Gard said. "Pay that too, and we'll talk."

"You can't be serious," Viola said.

"From an analysis of his vocal patterns," Puk said. "I gauge the likelihood of him being serious at 95%."

"Your bot's annoying," Gard said. "But it's not wrong. Double the coin. Then you get your boy back."

"I'll have to talk to Eden," Viola said.

"Take your time," Gard replied. "Morris isn't going anywhere."

Looking down the hallway, Viola noticed a pair of bouncers coming back through, another man in tow. The same one that'd been at Kassana's table pounding drinks. At a fork in the hall in front of them, the two bouncers turned right, dragging the drunk after them.

"When you get the coin, you just come back and find me," Kassana said. "We'll get it all taken care of."

They passed by the branch and Viola glanced down the hallway. The two bouncers were shoving the drunk man into a room. Along either side were sets of doors. It seemed likely Morris was in one of them.

"What're you thinking, Puk?" Viola said.

"The odds are terrible. But that's never stopped us before," Puk replied.

"What are you two talking about?" Kassana said.

#

Viola burst down the fork, towards the two bouncers, Puk following.

"What are you doing?" Kassana called. Her voice caused the bouncers to turn around, one slapping a panel on the side of the hall and closing the drunk's new home.

"Take them out," Viola said. "Gently."

"I can use my toys?" Puk said.

"Just this once."

The bouncers moved to meet them, but as they closed, Puk armed itself. Brought out the small laser embedded in its right side and fired once, twice. Bolts just powerful enough to overload a man's nervous system. Each shot hit its target in the face, and they fell to the ground. Viola knelt down and grabbed one of their stun batons, flipped a small switch at the base to turn on the electricity, and then zapped the bouncers with a light tap. Just to make sure.

"You two are insane," Kassana said. "Gard's going to kill you."

"Puk?" Viola said as Kassana turned to run. "She keeps moving, you stun her."

"Please," Puk said to Kassana. "Run."

The card dealer stood still, her hands raised. A good call. Viola grabbed one of the bouncers' wrists and pulled out her multi-tool. Flipped out the las-cutter, a two centimeter long super-hot beam, and, with a bit of precise slicing, cut the bouncer's comm off its owner. Then she slapped the comm against each of the scanners in the hallway in turn. Opening one door after the next until she found Morris. He was lying on the floor, still stunned from the batons. She'd have to carry him. Unless...

Behind her, the drunk man wandered out of his cell. Two other inmates did the same, looking at the downed bouncers. And then they ran.

"At least it's a distraction," Viola said. She looked at Morris, his tired jacket going with the standard issue forest green Eden pants. "Puk, get in here. Bring her."

The bot and Kassana entered a moment later. The card dealer had a look of permanent fear on her face. Like she could see her career draining away.

"You've got to have adrenaline here," Viola said. "Where?"

The chemical would kick-start anyone who'd been stunned. Jolt the body back to life. If they were going to run out of here, Viola needed Morris standing.

"It's back with Gard. Where they keep all the emergency stuff," Kassana said.

"Then I guess we're going back."

Viola led the way, holding the stun baton. Down to the branch in the hallway and then to the right, towards the lounge with the monitors. Everything was deserted, except for two people watching the screens. And on those screens, Viola saw why.

Out in *The Fools Chance*, chaos reigned. The people that'd skipped out of their cells were running around, trying to avoid Gard and the other bouncers. Knocking things over, throwing punches, and ruining games.

"Nice work," Puk said. The comment caused the two monitors to turn around, one started to raise his voice, and then he noticed Puk's laser.

"That's right," Viola said to the man. "The adrenaline? Where is it?"

The monitor pointed to a slot underneath the main wall of screens where, separated by a slight gap, sat a sealed box. Viola looked for a scanner, but didn't see one. Just a number pad. But without the code, there wasn't going to be a way to crack it. Not before they ran out of time.

"Either of you know the number?" Viola asked the monitors. They both shook their heads.

"Oh, I do," Kassana said. "All the dealers get it. In case we need a fix."

"Mind spilling it?" Viola said.

"If we make a deal," Kassana replied. "You get me off the *Lucky Star*, to anywhere else. And give me some of that Eden coin."

"Done," Viola said. It wasn't her coin. And she could drop Kassana off at Eden's own station, where the company's reps could take care of the dealer however they chose.

"Seven-seven-five-two," Kassana said, and Viola punched in the numbers. The box cracked open, revealing a bundle of adrenaline as well as a bevy of other drugs. The kinds of things that would keep people awake and moving long after their bodies wanted to shut down. Other, more illicit numbers, filled out the safe. Good to see the *Lucky Star* living up to its dubious reputation.

Viola grabbed the adrenaline and ran down the hall. Behind her, Viola heard Kassana reach into the safe and pulled out some clinking phials before following, feet pounding on the metal floor.

#

Viola inserted the needle into Morris's chest and pressed down on the plunger. A second later the man's eyes shot open and he gasped a loud, angry breath. And then his hands wrapped around Viola's throat.

"I'm from Eden," Viola coughed. "Here to get you out. Let go of me."

Morris looked at her sideways, his eyes narrowing. Then he let her loose. Viola stood up and stepped away, rubbing her neck.

"That how you treat everyone that helps you?" Viola said.

"Might be why he was drinking alone," Puk said.

"Always a little jerky when I wake up from a stunning," Morris said, standing up. Then he caught a view of who else was in the room. Puk, he ignored. But Kassana...

"Now Morris, darling," Kassana began. "I was helping..."

"You were helping?" Morris took three steps, towering over Kassana. "You were helping who? Yourself? Let me show you my appreciation."

Morris cocked back a fist and Kassana threw her hands over her face.

Puk flew in between. "With all due respect, Captain Morris, there will be time for revenge later. Our odds of getting out are going down with every second."

The blast of logic seemed to tone Morris down, and he lowered his arm. "Fine. Let's go."

Viola followed Morris out of the room, Puk and Kassana trailing behind. As they went by the bouncers, Morris bent and picked up the other stun baton. Halfway down the hallway, he turned and looked back at Kassana.

"She's not coming with," Morris said.

"She helped us get you up," Viola said. "We made a deal."

"I didn't. She's the reason I was stunned in the first place," Morris said, throwing fiery eyes at Kassana. "You tell them how you cheated me out?"

"I..." Kassana started. And ended as two more bouncers, carrying a limp, stunned escapee came around the corner. At the sight of Morris and the others, the bouncers dropped their prisoner. One started to bring his comm up to his mouth. Morris threw his baton. It spun through the air and struck the bouncer in the face.

The second bouncer didn't have time to react before Morris was on him, a blur of swinging fists and guttural growls. Viola stood and watched.

"He's pretty good," Puk said.

"I bet he gets in a lot of fights," Viola replied.

"All the time," Kassana said.

Ten seconds later they were moving down the hall again, the two new bouncers unconscious in their wake, lying next to their prisoner. They went through the red-lit door and back into *The Fool's Chance*. Morris seemed to be ignoring Kassana for the moment. Viola figured the captain had reordered his priorities, but she couldn't really tell, because the only thing Morris was doing was grumbling about cheaters and rubbing his bruised knuckles.

The Fool's Chance wasn't going to give them another opportunity to talk. It was a mess, with shattered glass, turned over tables, and a sloppy melee between gamblers, bouncers, and what passed for the *Lucky Star*'s general security. Gard was there in the middle of it all, his own fists flying.

Viola couldn't wait to get off of this station.

#

The four of them edged their way around the outside of bar floor, staying clear of the ongoing series of punches, kicks, thrown bottles and yells of outrage. The front door was getting closer. Viola started to hope that maybe, just maybe, they'd actually get out of here.

Until Morris paused, the captain's eyes tracking back to the center of the bar where Gard had just jumped on the counter, hands directing security.

"Now that's a fight," Morris said, pausing to watch the flying fists and tumbling bodies.

"It's not ours," Viola replied.

"Not yet," Morris said.

"What does that mean?"

"I'll be quick. Just a few licks," Morris said. Before Viola could protest, Morris waded his way into the fight, seemingly picking a target at random. The first man he came across was part of the *Lucky Star*'s security detail, a stocky man covered in branded black body armor. As the enforcer turned, Morris decked him. Kept on walking.

"He seems competent," Puk said.

"He seems like a moron," Viola said.

"Close," Kassana added. "When he's a little less angry, though, Morris can be a lot of fun."

Morris ducked a pair of wild swings from another patron, then barreled into the man, hugging him beneath his shoulders and using the guy as a battering ram to get through the crowd. Slammed the luckless man into the bar counter and let him drop. Turned and took a swipe at a bouncer who, tragically, failed to notice the loose cannon captain running wild behind him.

"What he said about cheating earlier?" Viola asked, watching the melee. "What was that about?"

"I may have been under my quota," Kassana said. "Morris was being annoying, so maybe I flipped some cards. I didn't know it was his last coin."

"Isn't that illegal?" Puk said.

"You know where you are?"

"Point."

Gard looked down from his post on top of the bar, noticed Morris beneath him. Shouted something that Viola couldn't hear, and then jumped down to the floor. Morris was ready, flew in with a right hook as soon as Gard hit the ground.

Only Gard wasn't slow either, his card-covered head ducking under Morris's punch. Gard delivered a pair of jabs into the captain's stomach, but Morris, either through the lingering supply of liquor in his blood, the adrenaline, or just pure rage shrugged them off, grabbed Gard by the shoulders and slammed him into the bar.

Gard rolled off the counter's edge, kept his balance, and when Morris moved in for the follow-up, Gard kicked a chair into Morris's legs. The captain tripped up over the plastic furniture and fell to the floor. Gard moved over to Morris, lifted up his foot, and fell over twitching.

"Get up," Viola said, holding the stun baton in her hand. "We're done here."

Morris untangled himself from the chair and stood, looked at Gard's unconscious form. "But I was having so much fun."

#

They were ten seconds into the *Lucky Star*'s corridor, heading towards the docking bay, before the shouts started.

"I think they've caught up to us," Puk beeped.

"Your bot is exceptionally competent at stating the obvious," Morris said. Behind them, back towards the bar, Viola noticed more *Lucky Star* security coming their way. These armed with more than stun batons.

"Helps keep me grounded," Viola said. "Puk, go get that shuttle ready."

Puk zipped out in front of them, floating over the heads in the crowded corridor. Kassana, Morris, and Viola dipped and dodged through the panicked people. Dealers and dopers dove all over the place, their wide eyes unsure if they were the targets. Viola tried to keep Morris in front of her, make sure the man wasn't going to dive off into another fight.

Stunning bolts shot through the crowd, knocking people to the ground. Viola held her focus, ducking and weaving at random. Fanning her jacket. Trying to be a hard target. They made it to the docking bay door, Morris stepping through and Viola right after. And then she heard the yelp. Even getting shot, Kassana's voice kept that silky strain.

"She's down," Viola called to Morris.

"Who cares?" Morris said, glancing out at Kassana's body. They only had a minute before security reached them.

"If it wasn't for her, you'd still be back in that cell," Viola said. "She made it even."

Morris huffed. "You're soft."

"Until we get back to Eden, I'm the leader on this mission. Carry her."

Was it reckless to risk Morris to save a card dealer? Maybe. But Viola did know that leaving Kassana here wouldn't be doing the woman any favors. Gard didn't seem the forgiving type.

Morris growled as a panicking gambler ran past the docking bay door. The captain reached out and grabbed the man. Held him in front of his own body as Morris stepped out from the docking bay. A series of stunning bolts slammed into the human shield, knocking the poor sap out.

Under the cover of the unconscious man, Morris moved closer to Kassana's body, reached out and grabbed her with one hand and dragged the woman along the ground.

As soon as they were back through the door, Viola shut the docking bay entrance and, activating the stun baton, jammed the weapon into the door's controls. She didn't know if it would actually do anything, but it didn't hurt to try. Puk lowered the shuttle's ramp and they, with Morris carrying Kassana, pounded up it.

Viola slid into the pilot seat and kicked the shuttle off the ground, up and out of the bay. Back into the infinite bliss of space.

"So what are we gonna do with her now?" Morris said, taking the copilot's chair.

"That's up to her," Viola said. "Where we're going, she'll have plenty of options."

"Where *are* we going?" Morris asked.

"Back where you belong," Viola replied.

Earth spread below them, and the *Lucky Star* drifted away behind the shuttle. As Viola punched in the flight path, she couldn't hold back a smile.

Maybe this job wouldn't be so boring after all.

-o-

A.R. Knight writes sci-fi and fantasy in the frozen north of Wisconsin. With a pair of cats keeping him company, he enjoys delving into adventures that are as much about the villain as the hero.

When he's not writing, he tends to travel anywhere he can, whether that's islands off the coast of Ecuador, the rainforest, snowboarding in the Rocky Mountains, or sipping scotch in Edinburgh. That's the nice thing about the writing life, you can take it anywhere.

Homepage: **http://adamrknight.com**
Mailing List: **http://adamrknight.com/newsletter**

There Comes a Time

by J J Green

When Caris came through, she fell to her knees on thick leaf mould. Her hands thudded into the ground before her, sinking into the damp, decaying surface. Humidity prickled her skin with sweat. She lifted her heavy head and tried to focus her swimming vision. Shades of green and brown danced and shimmered, then sharpened and slotted into perspective. She staggered up and checked behind her. Ferns, vines, trees, scattered pools and striations of light, the same as the scene in front. A din of cicada, frog and bird calls assaulted her ears. She rubbed her hands down her thighs and wiped the sweat from her face. One hour. First, she should try to find some clothes.

Caris was no expert on trees, but she guessed the largest ones she saw as she stepped through the jungle were more than forty to fifty years old. She was supposed to be in Stockbridge, Florida. Had they got the coordinates wrong? Or was it possible Stockbridge no longer existed? Without a trail to follow, she headed downhill. Downhill led to water, and water usually meant people.

She eased through the thick undergrowth. Damp foliage, branches and vines soon covered her bare skin in grime and a haphazard pattern of scratches, grazes. Hand-sized spiders hung suspended in webs between the trees, and snakes and lizards slithered and scattered at her approach. Rivulets of sweat cut tracks along her sooty skin.

The first building Caris saw appeared to rear up at her, it was so well hidden by the jungle. A half-crumbled wall, a vacant door and window frames collapsed and rotting. She stepped inside. The building was open to the sky. The remains of the roof littered the ground, and strong saplings sprouted among the cracked tiles and decayed timbers. She searched among the ruins. Anything and anyone that had once existed in the house was long gone. Nothing was there but dead leaves and the burgeoning life of the forest.

Caris wondered how much time had passed since she'd arrived. Half an hour? Forty-five minutes? She fumed at her superiors. What was she supposed to discover in just sixty minutes? Leaving the building, she surveyed the trees around her. One had a branch just above head height, and was taller than the others as well. She jumped and pulled herself up onto the branch. Grabbing vines, branches and knots she hauled herself up the tree until, balancing on a thin, springy branch and gripping fistfuls of shoots, she pushed through the canopy.

Sunlight pierced her eyes. Adjusting to the increased light, she became aware of a cloud of butterflies spanning the treetops as far as she could see. Floating, hovering, gliding; deep browns, purples and blacks shimmered, iridescent in the sunlight. Butterflies alighted on her, as if she were just another part of the canopy, and she grinned in delight. But puzzlement took over. Shading her eyes and looking into the far distance, all she could see was an ocean of leaves and butterflies like foam on the waves.

A sudden thought struck her. Was her hour nearly up? And if it was, she was about 75 feet above the ground. Would she be dragged back at the same height? She slid off the branch and descended rapidly, skittering monkey-like down the branches. Cursing as she acquired more scratches and bruises, she prepared mentally for a fall from mid-air. Fifty-foot drop. She might live if she fell from here. Twenty-five feet. She could get away with broken legs. Fifteen feet. If she executed a perfect roll, she might walk away.

They grabbed her as she jumped from the bottom branch. Caris' stomach lurched and her knees slammed into hard tile. Vomit forced its way up her throat. She spewed it out and pitched forward. Her head struck the floor and she slid through the pool of vomit in a dead faint.

#

"Should we contact someone? Husband? Relatives?" asked Lieutenant Merritt.

General Nancarrow shook his head. "She's single. No partner. No close relatives. That's one of the reasons she was chosen. Less chance of her letting something slip." The two army officers stood at Caris' bedside in a windowless hospital room.

"Okay, I'll ask the nurses to keep an eye on her so there's someone around when she wakes up."

"Thanks for taking over as her psych support at such short notice. We need to be careful. She'll most likely be groggy and disoriented. We can't risk her saying anything that sounds odd. You know what I mean. And we need her ready for debriefing as soon as possible. So stick around, is what I'm saying."

Merritt nodded and the general left. The lieutenant looked down at the unconscious figure on the bed. She had short hair and her thin face was bruised and scratched. She didn't look at all like his mental image of a time traveller, tough, exotic and strange. She looked very ordinary and vulnerable.

A screen was embedded on the wall next to the bed, and Merritt scrolled through the information. Twenty-six years old. Parents dead, one from a drug overdose and the other in a bank hold up, as the perpetrator. Foster care kid in numerous homes. Enlisted at sixteen. Exemplary record of active service. Prodigious technical talent. Merritt scrolled ahead to the psych evaluation. He scanned it, and went back to the personal history. Strange. Her psych score was nearly perfect, which was completely at odds with her upbringing.

He glanced down at Caris and started. Her eyes were open and watching him.

"See anything interesting?"

"Hi, Caris. Glad to see you're awake. I'm Lieutenant Merritt." He took out his ID and showed it to her. "I'm here to make sure you're okay. How are you feeling?"

"Like death."

Merritt drew up a chair and sat down. "It'll ease over the next few days, I expect. Time travel must be like an exaggerated version of long haul flights. You're experiencing a form of jet lag. Or time lag,

I suppose I should say."

"Hmph. So... you aren't a medic. You're the new psychiatrist?"

"Psych support officer. Hungry?"

"Nope. What happened to Lieutenant Norris?"

"He's in intensive care. Stroke. Thirsty? How about a drink?"

"That's for me, right?" Caris looked at the jug of water and tumbler on the table next to her bed. "I'll be okay." There was a silence. "Look, you don't have to hang around. I'm okay. I won't say anything to anyone, if that's what's worrying you."

Merritt stood up to leave, but hesitated.

"Really, I'm okay," said Caris. "I'm sure you have plenty to do."

Merritt leaned toward her and said in a low voice, "Caris, you've just been a hundred years into the future. Don't you want to talk about how you're feeling? You know, share? It must have been quite an experience."

Caris thought a moment then said, "No, I'm good."

Merritt tilted his head and smiled. The woman seemed perfectly calm and relaxed. He regarded her battered face. Gel coated the worst cuts, holding the edges together and healing them. In a few days' time, under the hospital's state-of-the-art care, she would be as good as new. And the physical effects of the first extended journey in time would have left as few effects on her body as it appeared to have left on her mind.

"You sure you don't need anything?"

Caris shook her head, smiled and gave Merritt a thumbs-up.

The next time he saw her was at the debriefing. She stood in uniform before an assembly of most of the highest-ranking military personnel in the country. Merritt scrutinized her facial expression and body language. She appeared entirely unfazed.

Nancarrow stood and turned to the other officers. "I propose we let Warrant Officer Elliott tell us her account, then ask questions. Are we in agreement?"

Caris spoke for twenty minutes, giving each detail of her experience from start to finish, describing the physical geography, flora and fauna she encountered, the single, tumble-down building she had found, and the view of endless jungle she had seen. A tutting admiral interrupted.

"There's surely been some kind of error here. That sounds nothing at all like Stockbridge. Is there something wrong in the calculations, or a problem with the machine? We must have sent her somewhere different. We sent her to the Amazon, or some such other place."

Nancarrow stood again. "Can we wait for Warrant Officer Elliot to finish?"

"General Nancarrow, I'm done. It was at that moment I was retrieved," said Caris.

"Right. Thank you, Corporal. Well, let's commence questions, then."

Merritt watched Caris. The officers fired off questions, interrupting one another and repeating themselves. The volume of noise in the room rose and petty squabbles broke out as each tried to make him- or herself heard. A heated argument on the possibility of global warming creating a jungle in the area broke out. Caris answered each question patiently, giving the same information over and over again. Merritt would have expected anyone else to experience frustration, but Caris only looked bored.

He took her back to the hospital for a final physical exam before she was discharged. The autocab whipped through the streets, equidistant from every other vehicle.

"Caris, I have a question for you about your experience, if you don't mind."

"Shoot."

"How did you feel about it?"

Caris sighed. "Look, I know you're just doing your job, but I'm okay. I'm not going to have a mental breakdown or anything. I'm not like that."

"I know. I'm your psych support, remember? I didn't mean that. I meant, what was it like, being there? A hundred years in the future. I mean, wow."

"Hmph." Caris watched the streets of Stockbridge fleeting past. Clean, neat, sharp-edged and modern. Glass-fronted stores glinted in the sunlight. The pavements were even, the signs bright. She thought back to the expanse of jungle that, as far as she could tell, would take its place in one hundred year's time. She turned to Merritt. "You know what? I felt great. It was beautiful."

"Yeah?"

"Yeah. It was alive, you know? So alive. I've never seen anything like it. It was how it must have been before we took over the planet. It's kind of nice to know there comes a time when we return the Earth to a natural state."

Merritt tried to imagine.

"Hey, you're okay, you know," said Caris.

"Huh?"

"The rest of them, they didn't care. All they wanted to know was where all the people had gone. No one else tried to understand what it was like. How it felt to be there."

#

The second time they sent her she had two hours. A pig, a dog and a monkey had survived four hours in the future, so there was no reason to suppose a human wouldn't survive half that, they had reasoned and she had agreed. Caris sat down to be transported. The last thing she saw was Lieutenant Merritt's face through the observation screen. He looked anxious, poor guy. Anyone would think it was him travelling into the future. Then came the dizziness and blurred vision.

The Stockbridge of fifty years hence surrounded Caris. It was a wrecked town. The buildings that were still standing were advanced in the process of disintegration. Weeds and saplings opened wide cracks in the sidewalk and roads. Concluding it wouldn't be safe to enter any buildings, as they all seemed in a state of imminent collapse, she leaned in through the windows. Rats scuttled away at her approach.

Apart from the rats, the place seemed devoid of life. It was silent and nothing moved in the streets. Caris walked to the places she knew, the sun hot on her skin. The sports stadium was a shell and the shopping center had clearly at some point collapsed in spectacular fashion. Now it was little more than a heap of concrete blocks, glass, rusting girders and dust. She remembered a small post office a few blocks downtown and headed there.

What remained of the post office was in no firmer state than the other buildings, but Caris had to risk entering it if she wanted to try and find out what had happened. Piles of yellowed, decaying papers covered the floor. Letters, postcards, bills, advertising. She dug down to reach less weathered paper on the lower layers, but they were sodden mush. The print on the papers on top was so worn and rain-damaged it was illegible. Caris lifted telephone receivers and listened to the silence. The computer screens were dead and cracked, the wiring rotten.

Caris estimated she had about forty-five minutes left. Enough time to get to the government buildings if she ran. Her orders were to bring back information on future technologies and survey the broader aspects of civilian life. If there was anyone left at all, they could be there. She ran through the empty streets, the sound of her footsteps echoing from the vacant, desolate buildings. A faint tingle of unease ran down her spine. The absence of life intruded into her senses, and the hairs rose on her neck. The empty windows seemed full of eyes, watching her. What had happened to all the people? Where had they gone? The derelict buildings seemed to be burgeoning with their ghosts, willing her to find out.

Caris stopped, resting her hands on her knees. She closed her eyes and shook her head. She stood straight and looked around at the buildings, willing the illusion away. Closing their eyes, the ghosts retreated.

In another five minutes she was at the central offices. The wide glass doors had shattered and glass crumbs adorned the grassy weeds growing through the sidewalk. Placing her bare feet carefully, Caris stepped inside. The ground floor had retained its ceiling, and the interior was dark. Caris waited a moment to allow her eyes to adjust, but she knew she had only a few minutes left. Squinting into the shadows, she walked through the reception area. Her foot caught, and she stumbled. Turning back to see what had tripped her, she gasped. Rotten clothes hung from a skeleton. She stood, and swiveled, surveying the room. Similar heaps were scattered across it. Bones and skulls, yellowed and stained, made disorganized piles on the floor. Caris' hackles rose as she felt herself grabbed back.

After the vomiting came oblivion.

#

Merritt offered to take Caris out to eat after the debriefing, and he wasn't surprised when she accepted. Her demeanor was altered, and it wasn't due to the arguing, shouting and chaos of the meeting. She was preoccupied and anxious, and he noticed her hands trembled. She was as laconic at dinner as she had ever been, however, and they ate in silence for a while.

"You want to talk about it?" he asked. When she didn't hear his question for the second time, he placed his hand on hers.

"Hey," she said, pulling her hand away.

Merritt raised his hands. "Just trying to get your attention."

"Oh. Sorry."

"It sometimes helps to talk things through. "

Caris sighed and closed her eyes. "I know. I do know that. It's just I'm not used to..."

"...feeling bad about stuff?" Merritt offered.

"Feeling bad about stuff. That's a good way of putting it."

"It's normal. Hell, if I'd been thrown into the future and dragged back again I'd be a wreck."

"Lieutenant Merritt..."

"Call me Ben."

"Ben," she said. "Ben, I've seen death. I've seen it happen to enemies and to friends. And I've stared it right in the face. Death's terrible, you know, but it is what it is. It comes to all of us. But there... that place... Ben, there was nothing. Nothing but rats, and silence." She shuddered. "And it's the future. That's what's coming, right?"

"No one knows, Caris. It's a possible future, certainly. But we don't know whether it's the only one. Some theories say time is already complete and part of the physical universe... that we're only experiencing the illusion of travelling through it. Others say there are multitudes of futures, each decided whenever there's a choice of possibilities. That's one of the things they're trying to find out, by sending people like you through. Only..."

"What?"

"The individuals that go through must be psychologically robust. You know the transporter only works for living things, so you can't take any recording equipment with you, and you can't bring any artifacts back. The reports you give must be reliable, and not influenced by your mental state..."

"Are you telling me I'm not fit to take the next run?"

"Caris, no one even knows whether there will be another run."

"I'm fine, Ben. I'm fine. Come on, don't tell them I'm not fit. You should have seen that place. We've got to find out what happened. So we can stop it happening. Don't tell them I'm not fit, please."

"Caris, as far as I'm concerned you're experiencing a normal reaction to what you saw. You just need to talk it through. I don't think you're unstable at all. But... talk, okay?"

While the President, the Cabinet, the generals and admirals debated and argued over how to proceed with investigating the future, Caris and Ben met daily for counselling sessions. Caris talked about what she had seen and how she had felt in the future Stockbridge, about her time in the army, the tours she'd been on, and her childhood going from foster home to foster home.

"Do you want to talk about how it felt? A new home, a new family every year or even more often?" asked Ben one day.

Caris shrugged. "It wasn't so bad. They were okay—the foster parents, I mean. Others had it worse than me."

Ben laughed and put down his pen.

"Did I say something funny?" asked Caris.

"Caris, I'm sorry. I'm not laughing at you, but I just don't understand how you've coped so well with everything that's happened to you. I've counselled soldiers with severe psychological disorders, PTSD, the works. And they haven't experienced half the trauma you have. I don't get it."

Caris looked out the counselling office window. "I don't know, Ben. Maybe it's different for some people. Maybe my experiences brought out the best in me. Maybe if I'd had an easy life I'd be a wreck."

"It's an interesting idea. And it's interesting talking to you, Caris."

She smiled and he smiled back. Their eyes locked a fraction too long, then they both looked away.

"You know, Ben, I never really understood the point of counselling before," Caris said. "but I needed these sessions, after my last assignment. They've helped."

Ben looked down at his notes.

"Is something wrong?" asked Caris.

"Caris, please believe me when I say it's nothing to do with anything you've said or done, but I have to step down as your counsellor. I'll find a replacement for you. A good one."

"What? Why? If it isn't me, why are you stepping down? What's wrong?"

"I'm afraid my professional code forbids me telling you that."

"Then don't tell me as my counsellor. Tell me as a friend."

"Caris, I can't be your friend, either."

Caris looked at Ben across the low coffee table that separated them. Moments passed, and he refused to meet her gaze. She got up, walked halfway to the door, then stopped. She walked back and stood next to Ben's chair. As he looked up at her, opening his mouth to speak, she stooped and kissed him.

#

A low moaning was the first thing Caris heard when she went through the third time. Ben's smiling face through the transporter room glass was still in her mind as, blinking her vision clear, she saw movement ahead. A beggar, staggering toward her. She sidestepped, but he grabbed her arm and pushed his face into hers.

"Help, help me," he breathed.

Caris turned her head to escape his foul exhalation and grabbed his arms to hold him away from her. She looked around, but the street was empty except for the two of them. She pushed the beggar gently away and stepped back.

"I'm sorry, but, as you can see, I need to find some clothes." She walked quickly away. When she had turned a corner, she slipped down the side path next to a house with no cars on the drive. Trying the back door, she was surprised to find it open. The house was empty, and it looked as though the family had left in a hurry. Dishes thick with mould filled the sink, and an unemptied rubbish bin sent out a stench. Upstairs, she put on clothes she found among the many left in the open wardrobes.

She looked out the bedroom window. It was about three in the afternoon but the street was empty. No one in the yards, no cars, no pedestrians, not even any kids playing on the sidewalk. Caris felt her knees buckle and she sat down on the unmade bed. The beggar, the hastily vacated house, the deserted street. This was only two years in the future. Whatever disaster was going to befall them, it was going to happen within two years. They had two years left?

For a while, Caris sat on the bed, unable to move. She looked out at the blue sky, sunshine and clouds, the silence pounding her ears. Then she stirred. Perhaps, if she could find out what had happened, they could put it right. They might be able to prevent the disaster happening. Ben had said there might be many possible futures. She needed to make at least one future safe.

She ran down the stairs and found the home computer, but it was dead. She flipped a light switch and cursed. The electricity was off. She could not access the autocab system even if it was still running. She would have to travel on foot again.

Caris jogged from house to house, knocking at doors and peering in windows. At one place two dogs barked and yelped. The sun sank lower. Caris ran through street after street. She could not find a single human being. Then she saw the front door to a house standing open. As she drew nearer, she smelled a terrible stench. She knew what it meant, but went inside to investigate anyway.

Downstairs was empty, so she went up to the bedrooms. A busy hum of flies came from the master bedroom. A brief look inside revealed what might once have been an old couple, lying in each others' arms. She ran to the next house. The front door was unlocked. Opening it, she was greeted with the same stench, and at the next house, and the next.

Caris ran down the street. She stopped and sank to her knees. For a moment she hugged herself, rocking, then forced herself to her feet. Blinking back tears, she looked around, got her bearings, then set off at a sprint. As she neared the hospital, she noticed banners draped across the signs. Hospital full, they said, in large, capital letters. Please return home. Wait for assistance.

Panting, Caris slowed to a walk. The hospital grounds were deserted. The ambulance bay was open. The automatic doors to the reception area stood apart. Caris stepped through and a nurse in a surgical mask and dirty scrubs ran up.

"Who are you? Have you come from the government? Have you brought supplies? Are they going to turn the electricity back on?"

"I... No, I'm sorry."

"You're a patient? We can't take any more. We can't help you. You have to go home."

"I'm not a patient. I just want to know what's going on."

"You want to... Where have you been?" The nurse's eyes grew wide above her mask. "If you haven't been in contact with anyone, you might stand a chance. Get away. Get away now. Go back wherever you came from."

"Please. Tell me what's happening first."

"It's a virus. It takes a few months to kill you, but it's deadly, and extremely contagious. Skin contact, breath, anything. No one knows where it came from, but it started here in Stockbridge and it's spreading everywhere. If you haven't touched anyone with it, you might be okay."

"If I haven't... " Caris remembered the beggar. "No. No... "She looked at the sun. How long did she have? Five minutes? Ten? She pushed past the nurse.

"Don't touch me! Where are you going?"

Caris started stripping her clothes. "I need a pen. And a scalpel."

#

Ben waited for Caris to reappear. Two hours in the future didn't mean anything in the present. For him, it had only been five minutes since she left. One second the transporter was empty; the next, she was there. He stared. She was lying on the floor, writing covering her from head to toe. Blood seeped from her wrists. The guards at the door tried to stop him but he was too fast. He shoved them aside and ran into the room. He grabbed Caris' limp form and pulled her into his arms. Her face and lips were white, lifeless.

"Caris..."

He heard a voice vaguely. "Step back, Lieutenant."

Hands pulled at him, dragging him away. Caris' body slipped from his grasp and slid onto the floor, her head lolling.

He tried to speak but nothing would come out. Avoiding Caris' glazed, vacant eyes, he read the writing on her body. It made no sense. The same three words written over and over again.

Don't touch me. Don't touch me. Don't touch me.

-o-

J.J. Green was born in London's East End within the sound of the church bells of St. Mary Le Bow, Cheapside, which makes her a bona fide Cockney. She first left the U.K. as a young adult and has lived in Australia and Laos. She currently lives in Taipei, Taiwan, where she entertains the locals with her efforts to learn Mandarin.

Homepage: **http://jjgreenauthor.com**

Red Fortitude

by Eddie R Hicks

Every sense in your body is heightened when you enter the cold vacuum of space. Especially if you're alone. Captain Jessica "Aura" Davis' body performed a quick turn to reorient herself. The burgundy horizon of Mars appeared seconds later through the helmet of her space suit. Sunlight in the distance shined through the visor of her helmet, casting its light across her smooth ebony face. The holographic HUD inside relayed white and blue imaginary of the surrounding area and the location of the elusive beacon she spent the last four hours searching for.

She took several deep breaths, triggering her mind to focus on the next hurdle. *Stay calm and focused, almost done.* She looked around once more, no ships, no other United Nations of Earth (UNE) personnel. She was alone. Her left hand rose up and lightly and tapped the flag of the United Kingdom on her shoulder, a good luck ritual of hers, before she activated the jet pack on her suit. Its thrusting force of indigo energy propelled her body towards Mars, and towards the pulsing beacon.

"I got this!" a man spoke over the radio with a southern American accent.

So much for being alone, she thought and then located the person in question on her HUD. There was indeed another target approaching the beacon according to the blue blip that appeared at the end of the projection. "You're coming in too fast," Jessica transmitted to him.

She remained on course, her suit providing just enough thrust towards the beacon but not too much that she'll overshoot it when she arrives. Unlike the American of the distance, coming in way too fast, at this rate he'll slam right into it, if he's lucky. She saw him quickly approach, as he cut the jets from his suit. His hands reached out to grab a hold of the beacon... and missed. His leg, however, didn't. The impact that followed flung his body away, spiraling out of control towards Mars.

"Aw hell, what did I tell you?" she said to him. He replied back over the radio with laughter. "Oh bloody hell, hang on."

When the time was right, Jessica cut the thrusts from her suit, and allowed the light forward momentum to carry her towards the beacon. She held onto the floating satellite hard as it came close, causing her body to slowdown. Her fingers imputed a sequence of command codes onto an exposed console. A light on the beacon began to pulse green rapidly shortly afterwards. *It's done, finally.*

Now for the next task at hand. The man in the suit from earlier continued to spiral out of control, and would continue to do so until his movement stabilized so that he could use jets properly. She released her grip on the beacon, aimed her body, and then primed her jets once again, launching her on a direct course towards him. Her hands extended forward as she neared him to offer assistance. His tumble stopped as the two held onto each other. Once the two were stable, her retro rockets fired to decelerate them.

"I'm not gonna lie," he said to her. "That was awesome!"

"It's called survival training not orbital training..."

The last beacon was finally activated putting an end to their training for the day. Five minutes later, multiple transports accelerated towards the two from the opposite end of Mars. Various other UNE personal also adrift in Mars' orbit during the training run were also picked up.

#

Ares Station Gamma was one of four orbiting UNE military space stations around Mars. This station in particular hosted UNE pilots for their twelve week survival training session, a brand new and mandatory program that everyone enlisted must participate in. It was a program Jessica wasn't exactly fond of.

Most of her childhood in some way was a never ending survival training session. At eight years old she found herself an orphan roaming the streets of Manchester, what was left of it, in the aftermath of the Hashmedai Empire's invasion of Earth. There wasn't much in terms of order back then; if alien invaders weren't trying to kill you, then looters in the streets were. She learned quite a bit about survival then, and additional things when Martin Xavier found her and raised her in the years that came.

Speaking of him, Jessica thought as she finished putting her uniform on. A small computer inside of her quarters chimed; there was an incoming transmission for her. And there was only one person that would want to speak with her in private.

She tied her black hair into a pony tail before picking up the message. A small hologram of her foster father appeared. He began to speak after a small five second communication delay. "Jessica my dear, great to see your face again."

"A live transmission, you must be close by?"

"Aye, the *Wilfrid Laurier* is making a flyby. Figured I'd send ya a live message rather than those boring recorded ones," he said. "How's the training coming along?"

"Finished the space part, Mars is up next."

"You'll do just fine, just watch out for those goddamn sandstorms," he said after an eight second delay.

"The delay is getting longer."

"Must be moving further outta range. Well, I'll let you get back to it, good luck, and stay safe."

It's a shame the transmission had to end so quickly. She missed the many stories he had to tell about his early days in the Royal Navy, and what life was like before the human race discovered the existence of alien life. It was stories like that influenced her to enlist and join the UNE forces and become the fighter pilot she was today.

Later in the day, she entered the mess hall... alone. It was reasonably packed with pilots all awaiting their next trials in their mandatory survival training. It was hard to make out what some people were saying giving the various languages being spoken.

German, Italian, Japanese, Russian, Hindi, English... the UNE recruited from across the globe. It's amazing what the human race could accomplish when you ignore borders and work towards a common goal, defending Earth from future alien invasions.

A familiar face bumped into her as she filled her meal tray with a hearty selection of food. First Lieutenant Greg "Hammer" McTavish, an accomplished pilot she'd met during her brief stay at the UNE base in New Dublin.

"McTavish, wasn't expecting you out here," she said to him.

"Aye, been stuck here for the last two weeks, the team I was supposed to go down to Mars with failed the space survival tests."

"Odd one out, eh?"

"Pretty much. How about you, lass?"

"I'm the only one from my team in Geneva to get shipped out here. Only sendin' one of us at a time to ensure they still got people ready in case of an attack."

"Didn't realize our forces were stretched so thin."

"That's what happens when you move to colonize the whole solar system so fast."

The two sat down at a large nearby table. An observation window was behind them, delivering an awe-inspiring view of space and Mars in the distance. Perfect seats for partaking in the delightful task of indulging in their meal. *Way better than rations, the chef on this station has out done himself again.*

"Let's get a team together," Jessica said after finishing her steak.

"Thought ye'd never ask."

"I have no plans on staying on this station for weeks because people aren't capable of finishing the first test."

A young man with a meal tray had approached one of the many vacant sets next to the two. He had the American flag on his uniform and the rank insignia of a Second Lieutenant. "Mind if I join ya?" he asked, his accent... southern American.

"You're that recruit from yesterday..." Jessica said to him.

"The one spiraling in orbit around Mars? Hell yeah, that was me."

"Your accent isn't hard to miss."

"Accent? Ain't you the one with the accent, lovely Brit one at that." He sat down next to her, and then offered his hand for a formal hand shake. "Name's Fisher, Mike Fisher."

"Jessica Davis..." she said shaking his hand. "Nice to meet you, now that you're not in orbit."

"Just won't live that down eh?"

"I suppose I'll let it go in time. Command on the other hand..."

"Meh, ain't worried about them, the training on Mars, that's where all the points are at," Fisher said. "We're all pilots anyways, ain't no reason for us to learn how to survive in the vacuum of space. Hell, I reckon in a few years they'll scrap this whole program all together, train people what they need to know when it comes to survivin'."

"Are you daft? It's all important," said Jessica.

"If our fighter gets shot to hell, we'll eject into an escape pod."

"The escape pods on our fighters have no atmosphere like our cockpits. The pod is just to send a beacon and protect you from debris and radiation if you end up spending a long time adrift."

"So shouldn't they be teaching us how to survive in a pod rather than being out in space activating beacons, 'cause reasons?"

"Our flight training covers the use of the escape pod."

"Exactly!" Fisher jubilantly shouted. "All this is pointless."

"Look, everyone is expected to go through the same training, survival in space with only a suit, and then survival on Mars."

"I just want this done and over with, apparently you can't advance through the ranks until this training is finished."

Jessica smiled for a moment, having made captain before the survival training plan was made mandatory. Had she enlisted later, she would have had to perform this training straight after finishing basic.

"So you're a new recruit?" she asked Fisher.

"Yes ma'am, eager to get this over with so I can get my butt into a flight simulator."

"What's wrong?" McTavish cut in. "Don't like being a transport pilot?"

"Ain't what I signed up for, sir," Fisher replied, then pointed toward the window behind them looking out into space. A squad of *Solaris* fighters flying in formation on patrol could be seen making a pass by the window. "That's where the action is, and if those Hashmedai ever come back, we'll be the ones pushing them back into space."

Their brief chit chat came to an end as a six person group of pilots arrived at their table. None of them looked happy, especially their leader who stood with her arms crossed seemingly unimpressed. Jessica recognized her, Asian woman with her hair tied into a pony tail. It was the infamous Captain Meifeng "Red Lotus" Lin, part of the Hyperion squadron assigned to Titan.

"Do I amuse you?" Jessica asked Red Lotus who did nothing but gaze at the three.

"You're sitting in my chair, at our table," Red Lotus replied.

"Last time I checked, the mess is for everyone."

"This table is for us."

"Who's us?" McTavish asked.

"Hyperion squadron," Red Lotus said.

Both McTavish and Fisher kept silent.

"We were here first," Jessica said, defiantly. "I don't see your team's name on it, and was not told we had to leave otherwise. Find another table or wait for us to finish..."

"My team works hard and deserves the best seat," Red Lotus spoke down to Jessica. "We shouldn't have to be forced to sit apart while every other team gets to sit and eat with each other. With that said, why not sit with your teams?"

"We aren't part of one..."

"Then do like the rest who are solo and sit in whatever vacant space you can find, Hyperion should not and will not sit in random spots because of you three."

Jessica rose up from her seat, the palms of her hands slammed against the metal surface of the table causing everyone in the mess hall to become silent and fix their eyes on her and Red Lotus.

"OK, I don't like ya attitude," Jessica said, then quickly stepped towards Red Lotus.

"What are you going to do about it?" Red Lotus said. "Now that you've gotten up, finish up with the last step, and step away..."

Thump. Jessica's sucker punch drilled into Red Lotus' face, sending her falling backwards. "Sorry love, did I just knock you on yer arse?"

Red Lotus' predicable retaliation came next, and the two entered a brief brawl. Jessica's actions weren't exactly the most professional way to handle things. But it was the most natural. One of the earliest lessons in life Martin taught her when they were salvaging for what they could find in the ruins of Manchester. Don't take any shit from anyone.

A few of the personnel in the mess hall stood and watched in shock, while others crowded around like it was a boxing match, cheering on the person they wanted to win. An airman from Red

Lotus' group pulled her back as McTavish pulled Jessica back, the message from them was clear enough, 'break it up.'

"OK, we'll find someplace else to sit..." McTavish said to Red Lotus.

"Like hell we will!" Jessica shouted, trying to break free of her friend's grip.

"Jess... please," McTavish pleaded.

It took Jessica some time, but she ended up standing down. Not because Red Lotus looked like she was going to do the same, or because of McTavish. But because she officially lost her appetite. Can't eat when you're pissed off at someone. That and her lip radiated with pain and dripped blood.

#

Jessica retreated to her quarters, a bottle of whisky helped keep her mood up in the aftermath of the disagreement, not to mention took her mind off the fact that the quarters next to her was playing some loud thumping music and overall being inconsiderate. Thankfully nothing else happened afterwards in regards to their skirmish. Red Lotus had too much pride to file a complaint; everyone else in the mess hall knew to stay out of everything Hyperion squadron was a part of.

She was about to take another hit of her drink, having not had one for the last hour, when an knock came on her door. Opening it revealed McTavish's presence as the lights from the hallway radiated across the top of his buzz cut hair.

"What were ya thinking, lass?" he said to her.

"I don't want to talk about it right now..." she said, inviting him inside. "That stunt really pisses me off."

"It's Hyperion..."

"Yeah, yeah, best of the best, protecting the furthest human settlement in the system, heard the speech; got the t-shirt, don't give a shit about them."

"Just be thankful everyone turned a blind eye towards this."

"We need to get our team made quickly," she said. "I'm not going to watch those elitist arses finish this training while we are stuck waiting for enough solo trainees to show up and slowly form a group."

"Four is the minimum, but command recommends six."

"Let's go with four and hope for the best," she picked up her holo pad and began to input their information into the screen; officially making them part of a team for the next leg of training. "You and I puts us at the halfway point, just need two more."

"How about that lad from earlier? He looked like a solo recruit."

"He's a bloody FNG," she said shaking her head.

"Beggars can't be choosy, especially in our position."

"I suppose you're right, if he's in that makes three... just need one more."

A loud muffled thud came from the room next to hers followed by drunken laugher and roaring. "Loud neighbors, eh?" he asked.

"Second bloody night in a row," she said flinging her holo pad onto her bed. "I've had enough."

She stormed off towards the door, McTavish followed behind, clearly concerned about how she was going to handle this next conflict with station personnel.

"Jess..." he mumbled to her.

She turned to face him with a warm smile before leaving, "I won't hit anyone this time!"

Jessica's fists knocked on the next door room; she hoped this would be the only time she'd have to use her fists to solve a problem. The source of the loud music and other forms of irritating racket began to drop in intensity. The sliding doors slithered open, a young woman with short red hair greeted her. There was some wobbling in her movement; she was drunk or at least getting to that stage. Inside were five other crew members from the station, drinking, yapping, and otherwise enjoying the small party. Some were fellow pilots, others were marines. There were no navy personnel. *Of course not, they're not that dense to partake in a party inside of someone's quarters.*

"Kinda full at the moment, but if they leave," the woman spoke. "We might be able to get you in!"

"Not here to party, here to file a noise complaint," said Jessica.

"We aren't that loud."

"I can hear all the high jinks you and your friends are causing! Besides I don't exactly think this is okay with Ops."

The party goers inside started to make their way to the exit after watching the small exchange between Jessica and their host.

"We were on our way out, ma'am," one of the marines inside said to Jessica. "Catch you later, Piller," he then said to the woman.

One after another, they all left, forcing the party to come to a close. Jessica figured her rank and tone of voice frightened them off. *Well that's one problem dealt with,* she thought. Though the quarters of the woman who was hosting this party however, wasn't up to spec; empty bottles and rubbish littered the floor.

Out from a nearby elevator stepped Red Lotus, of course it would be her. She looked furious as she moved directly towards the party that ended.

"Two times now I've been trying to read and noise from this room has interrupted me!" Red Lotus harshly roared to Piller.

Piller was slow to react, probably too drunk to realize that a superior was pissed off and wanted answers from her. Jessica cut in and said to Red Lotus. "That's nice, now go back to your book."

"Some of us are taking this training seriously; some of us are trying to get some sleep."

"That's nice," Jessica repeated. "Now go back to your quarters."

Red Lotus sighed. "People from Earth... nothing but trouble makers."

Seriously... Jessica thought as she and Red Lotus looked at each other with contempt. She had a hard time trying to let her comment go. The colonies throughout the solar system were still fairly new; most of the population at one point originated from Earth, before moving there. Red Lotus was no different. She may have lived on Titan, but was born on Earth, and if her comment was any indication, the folks on the colonies were already starting to make themselves feel different compared to their counter parts living on Earth.

If that's how it's going to be... "Clean up inside," Jessica said to Piller. Earthers are going to have to look after each other.

"I'll be fine," she said.

"No, do it now," Jessica said. She then faced McTavish. "Greg, give her hand please."

"Aye," he replied and entered her quarters.

As the doors slid shut, Red Lotus demanded to know, "What's going on in there?"

"Nothing you need to worry about," Jessica said to her. "Now leave. Don't you and Hyperion have to sing lullabies to each other or something?"

"Is there a problem?" said a voice neither of the two wanted to deal with. A voice of stern authority. The voice of General Landis.

Everyone in the halls stood at attention and the decorated gray haired general walked through, stopping right at the quarters both Jessica and Red Lotus stood at.

"Sir, no sir," Red Lotus replied back.

"I heard noise from two decks above," said Landis.

"Sir, we have it all under control," Jessica said.

"Do you now?" Landis asked, and then inputted his override code into the control panel for Piller's quarters.

Jessica began to come up with a long list of possible replies she could spit out when the general started to ask why the quarters in question looked like such a mess, like there was a party going on. From the corner of her eye she could see that... the rubbish was gone, and both McTavish and Piller remained calm. *Good job!*

"Captain Davis, Captain Lin," Landis said toward both Jessica and Red Lotus. "You two are the ranking officers in this section of the station, see to it there are no further disturbances."

"Yes sir!" they both said.

Everyone became at ease as the general walked away from sight. Red Lotus went back up to her quarters a minute later as both Piller and McTavish approached Jessica.

"Hey... thanks," she said to Jessica.

"No more high jinks, understood?"

"Understood ma'am. Just wanted to have a bit of fun before military life takes over. And do some networking, I'm all alone here."

"Not part of a team?"

"No, ma'am."

McTavish and Jessica looked at each other. He nodded to her with a grin and thumbs up. Jessica replied with a sigh and face palm.

"What's your name recruit?" Jessica asked her.

"Cassie Piller, second lieutenant."

Team member number four was found.

#

Three days later, two transports were primed and ready to launch as Jessica, Piller, McTavish and Fisher entered the launch bay. The four of them were officially registered as a team and ready to undertake the final survival training mission on the surface of Mars. They all wore environment suits, much like Red Lotus and her team, as they boarded the transport opposite of theirs.

Teams were dumped on the surface equipped with their environment suit and nothing else. Small shelters were deployed in random locations full of supplies, med kits and O2 tanks, and of course a somewhat comfortable atmosphere on the inside beyond the airlock. The goal was to survive with what limited resources you could find in the shelters for four weeks until the training ended. The location of the shelters were secret, the amount of supplies inside were random. You might get a stash that could keep your team alive for days; you might find a stash of food when you really needed medical supplies.

Most daunting part of it all? Communications were fixed so that you could only speak to people in close range. Needless to say, calling for help during an emergency was out of the question. If you were injured, command didn't know about it. The only link there was to the outside world were one's vital signs as they were transmitted to the station in orbit. If it looked like someone was about to die, or had died, then and only then would a rescue team be sent.

The all clear was given, and ships rose up and propelled out of the launch bay of the station and made their dive towards the red world below them. The loss of gravity was almost instant now that the transports were no longer bound by the artificial gravity of the station's rotating habitat rings.

Jessica saw the desert terrain of Mars via the forward windshield; they were quickly approaching. Large swirling clouds of dust and sand were starting to take shape. A storm was coming, a sand storm. "Figures they'd send us down during a sand storm," she commented.

"Wouldn't be a challenge without one," said McTavish.

"Visibility might be an ass, but walking through one shouldn't be an issue," she said. "It's the supply shelters; they're partly powered by solar power."

"So if we're low on air and can't get the systems inside to work..." Fisher said with a worried tone of voice.

"Aye, so let's not be in that position," Jessica said addressing her team.

As they neared the surface, gravity started to take hold of their bodies, forcing their feet to stay on the floor of the transport. Only, it was Martian gravity, instant sixty-two percent weight loss when compared to Earth.

Jessica got up to head to the rear section of the transport in anticipation of the doors swinging open. Hyperion squadron's transport exploded.

What remained of it plunged down towards Mars, leaving behind a trail of black smoke.

"The hell?" Jessica said toward the transport's pilot. "What's going on?"

"Looks like an explosion! They're going down."

She looked at the burning craft as it continued to spiral and crash. As much as she detested Red Lotus and her team, she didn't wish death on them. At the end of the day they were all UNE military personnel, they were on the same team. If they were going to die it should be on the field of battle against the enemies of the human race, not here on some damned survival training exercise.

A second blast rattled Jessica's ears; this one came from inside the transport she was on. Looking back behind her, she saw fires rage as smoke filled the cabin. Her team desperately tried to deal with the fire, but no avail. A secondary blast threw them all to the floor. Jessica's transport plunged towards the surface of Mars, on fire, triggered by an unknown explosion.

This was no accident...

"I'm losing control!" the pilot shouted.

"We're venting atmosphere!" Piller shouted.

Jessica turned around and saw that she was indeed right; the smoke was being sucked out by small holes along the walls and ceiling.

"Everyone, helmets on now!" Jessica said running towards the exit of the transport.

Her team all donned their helmets and began to take in the fresh breath of air the suit provided for their lungs. After the pilot applied his helmet he reported to the rest, "Brace for impact!"

"No," she said cutting the pilot off. "We won't survive the crash! Let's jump out now."

Jessica inputted a command on the wall terminal next the doors of the transport, the transport doors were forced open. The light red rue of the Martian horizon was the first thing she laid her eyes on. She was quite impressed on how calm everyone on her team remained during this critical situation, especially Fisher and Piller the FNGs.

She took a look down towards the red desert that grew in size; the sandstorm was quickly rolling in. Between the low gravity on Mars and the jet thrusts on their suits, their descent after leaping out from the burning craft shouldn't be fatal, at least that's what her suit's HUD reported.

She ordered everyone to jump out; one by one they leaped out and activated their jets to slow their fall. Jessica and the pilot remained, a pilot who still sat at his seat up front trying his best to keep the doomed craft still. She tried calling out to him, there was no reply, he wanted to keep the craft still and its crash to the surface controlled so that they could all leap out safely, or so she thought.

The transport rocked and slightly rolled, nearly causing Jessica to lose her footing. Now or never, she can't force him to save his life, and at this point her team below was going to need her to lead them out of this mess. She leaped out, and hoped that the pilot would clue in that it was his turn to do the same, or that she was wrong, and the crash was survivable.

Her jets powered on and her body slowly floated down to the surface like a prewar sky diver leaping out of a plane. The blue thrusts from her jets caused the sand below her feet to blow away as she safely came to a landing. She looked up at the track of black smoke in the air, it stretched out across the horizon, there were no signs of the pilot. The loud thud that came later signaled the transport crashing into the ground. Her HUD reported no signs of life within a fifty metre radius of her, and therefore nobody to communicate with due to training mission's survival settings. *Bullocks...*

Her traverse into the desert all alone, as a sandstorm rolled in, made her grimace behind her helmet. Sand, rocks, hills, more sand, howling winds blowing towards her. Every step she took to find her missing team put her closer into the mouth of the storm that looked like a giant cloud cruising across the surface. If the now dissipating smoke in the sky was any indication, she was walking towards the estimate location where the other three had leaped out to. Here's hoping they aren't walking in the opposite direction of her, otherwise this trek would turn into a quest of her chasing them down.

Visibility as well as light was low, she was directly inside of the storm now and it was giving her scanners a hard time. She nearly tripped over three different large rocks due to not seeing them and her HUD failing to relay to her that there was an obstacle nearby. It almost failed to report the existence of a person wearing an environment suit lying down on the dusty landscape. It was someone from the team, no question, but who? And were they alive?

"Hang in there, I see you," she transmitted to them now that she was in range. Nothing but static and garbled words back was their reply, *damn this storm!*

She got closer and knelt down beside the person. Communication strength started to improve, their voice became clearer, it was Fisher.

"Lieutenant," she addressed him while whipping way a layer of sand that covered the top of his visor.

"I'm fine," he said. "My leg on the other hand..."

Her HUD began a quick scan of his suit and the condition of it; there were clear signs of damage and worst of all. "You're leaking O2..."she reported.

"So that's what those alarms were..." he said then laughed. "My HUD is all messed up right now, probably damaged on impact."

"Hey!" Piller's static voice yelled.

Jessica looked away from Fisher, and saw Piller's body slowly emerge into visual range from the bluster of sand and dust. She waved towards Piller, signaling her to come towards the two of them and assist.

"He's got an hour of air left at best," Jessica said to Piller. "Here and here..." she pointed to the punctures in suit as they sprayed pressure, air and heat away. Piller's hands pressed down upon the damaged parts of his suit to slow the leakage of atmosphere. "That looks like where all the air is leaking out. Can you supply him with some air?"

"I can but..."

"It could be hours before we find the closest supply depot, I'd rather him be alive when we get there."

"I'm just gonna slow you all down, don't drag me along," Fisher said.

"I'll find it myself," Jessica said and stood up. "You two stay here and keep safe."

"What happened to the transport?" Piller asked.

"Both exploded from behind..." said Jessica.

"It was a bomb wasn't it?" asked Fisher. "What are they called? Hashmedai Liberation Front?"

HLF, the one group of lunatics that would place a bomb aboard a space craft, if they had the chance. "HLF? No way, they don't operate outside of Earth," Jessica concluded.

The HLF were made up of a group of Hashmedai who were left behind on Earth after the war had ended. Several humans began to take pity on them, alien soldiers who were stranded on a world that wasn't theirs. As time went on, those human sympathizers got close to those Hashmedai and formed the group. They launched a barrage of terrorist attacks, demanding that Hashmedai that were left behind be given the same rights and freedoms humans have.

"Who else could it have been?" Fisher asked.

"I'll be back," was all Jessica could reply with as she started her hike, taking her deeper into Mars' infamous tempest.

An hour had passed, Jessica nearly ran into the walls of one of the supply shelters. To her disappointment she got there too late, someone else managed to force the doors open and help themselves to the goods beyond the shelter's airlock. She hoped it was McTavish, the last person from her team that was uncounted.

"Hey," Jessica transmitted to them.

"Well what do we have here..." it was Red Lotus, of course.

"I need O2 tanks and a med kit," Jessica said to her. "One of my team members was hurt."

"I have five injured on my team," Red Lotus said, securing an O2 canister into her hands. "Sorry I can't spare anything."

"There's gotta be more inside."

"Command made sure these shelters were lightly stored to force us to be careful."

"I get that, but we got a critical situation here."

"I have a responsibility to my team," Red Lotus said and began to walk away with the goods in hand. "I have to get them out of this mess."

Jessica followed behind and said. "So do I, and one of them is going to die."

"If I give you this, I'll be asking two people to die," said Red Lotus. "This isn't the only supply stash, find the other and help your injured team mate, I'm sorry."

"How bad are your people?"

"All of their suits were damaged during the crash and leaking O2 as we speak. Some were burned while the others got some nasty cuts."

"What you got there isn't going to keep them alive for long."

"No it won't, until I find more supplies... or command realizes what happened." Jessica heard the tone of Red Lotus' voice switch to a more pleasant one. "Help me with my team... and I'll help you find another depot."

"Just like that?"

"As it stands, if we both don't find a second shelter, we're both going to lose people."

Jessica nodded and joined Red Lotus on her trek back to the crash site of her team's transport. "Let's move quickly."

#

Another hour passed and there were no signs of the storm letting up. Jessica and Red Lotus did what they could to patch up the suits of Hyperion squadron and kept them alive a little while longer with the O2 tanks supplied, before heading back into the unknown. Jessica wondered how everyone else was holding up, upon seeing the red holographic bars in her HUD that represented her air supply slowly shrivel away. Assuming Fisher wasn't dead, the air that Piller was sharing with him might be nearing critical levels. Those O2 tanks needed to be found and taken back to them quickly; no way in hell was she losing people under her command.

"Any idea what happened to the transports?" Jessica asked Red Lotus, breaking their nearly hour long silence during their journey.

"HLF bomb."

"That crossed my mind, but don't they operate on Earth?"

"They'll strike any UNE or Radiance target, it's just their resources are limited, and leaving Earth requires tough background checks."

"And half of the HLF are Hashmedai, it's impossible for them to leave Earth without being detected..."

"The transport we were on came from Earth."

"I know, they were the same ones I rode on to come here, from Geneva."

"The HLF that planned the bomb had to have come from Geneva as well, and had to have been on the transport."

Jessica was slightly baffled by Red Lotus' statement. "Explain..."

"Those weren't time bombs; they went off right as we entered Mars' atmosphere. It was planned, they wanted us to crash and they wanted the station to be intact. Otherwise they would have blown it up while it was still docked, and done a lot more damage."

"That's true, but why wait for us to head to Mars?"

"Because the terrorist was probably still on the station and didn't want to get killed themselves, they needed to the transport to be clear of it, they needed it to be close enough that they could survive the crash."

'They,' the implication being that someone on one of the transports was secretly a terrorist. Jessica didn't like where the conversation was heading, they needed to be focused on getting out of this alive, not pointing fingers at each other. "So you're saying someone from one of our transports is an HLF member."

"From what you told me, your pilot and one other is missing. You have two others that are brand new recruits from Earth, as in we know very little about them. Meanwhile my pilot is dead, and Hyperion squadron is from Titan, we haven't been to Earth in years. And you yourself said you're from Geneva. Do the math."

She should have become a detective not a fighter pilot. "We got no proof of that."

Thirty minutes later another sand-covered supply shelter came into view. As with the previous one, the doors had to be manually forced open due to the lack of solar power. They entered a small dark room as they passed through the airlock. Jessica hoped for the best as they started to plunder the supply crates inside.

Food rations.

Food rations.

Medical supplies, which will be needed to treat Fisher's wounds.

Food rations.

Food rations... *goddamn it.*

O2 tanks within the final crate, finally. Jessica grabbed three from the crate and then made her way towards the airlock. Quickly.

"I thought you needed one O2 tank?" Red Lotus asked her.

"Piller is supplying him with her own air," she replied. "We've been gone so long she might be low as well." She spun around and looked at Red Lotus' face as the lights from the inside of her helmet shined upon it. It was the look of someone that wasn't impressed. "Look, I'm not the terrorist if that's what's going through your head."

"I'm just worried you might be helping the person that put us in this spot."

Back outside, Jessica loaded a rough map of the area through her HUD. It displayed a record of everywhere she had been since setting

foot on Mars, including the last location where she left Piller and
Fisher. It took a while, but the computer was able to plot a course
directing her to where she needed to walk via a superimposed
holographic projection across her visor.

She took one step forward.

And was tackled to the rusty land below her by Red Lotus.

Multiple theories played out in her head. Red Lotus was really the
terrorist? Or perhaps she wanted the O2 tanks for herself. Or maybe
this was payback for the sucker punch from earlier?

Jessica was wrong on all accounts.

Multiple gun shots roared, every bullet flying towards the general
area she was standing prior to being tackled.

Jessica quickly got back to her feet, well as quickly as she could
with the Mars gravity and winds doing their things. She couldn't see
the gunman very well in the distance, but no shots were fired back at
her or Red Lotus as they ran behind the shelter for cover. Whoever
this person was, they were having a hard time getting a fix on their
location, the storm must be giving their eWeapon trouble, much like
how their suits were struggling to scan and communicate.

Jessica heard footsteps pressing against the sand. Someone was
creeping up towards them. Her first thought was it was the gunman,
but he was still a few metres away from what she'd seen. Even if he
ran could it be possible he'd be this close already? The steps were
coming from her left, and so she signaled to Red Lotus to move to
the right, around the circular structure they hid behind. With any
luck she might be able to get the jump on the person in question,
while Jessica remained here as bait.

There were sounds of a brief struggle, like someone got jumped.
Red Lotus? If it was her, she got there fast. The footsteps got closer.
It was multiple steps at that, at least two people, and Jessica
seriously doubted Red Lotus was one of them. She had to have been
moving around on the other end still. There were two people
approaching Jessica, McTavish and the pilot were the only ones not
accounted for. She took several deep breaths in preparation for
learning who was around the corner.

The two figures arrived in visual range at last; Jessica was forced
to stand up as she quickly figured out what was going on. The
gunman was one of the footsteps, he held a rifle to the back of the
head of another person. The face of McTavish was barely visible
from the visor.

"Give me the O2 tanks and you all get to walk," said the gunman, his voice was that of the missing pilot.

If Jessica resisted, both she, McTavish and possibly Red Lotus could end up dead, resulting in Fisher and Piller dying as well.

Option number one: Sacrifice the lives of Fisher and Piller, to save the three?

Option number two: Sacrifice the lives of superior officers so that the lower ranking ones can live.

"Damn it!" Jessica yelled as she held one of the O2 canisters up... while watching Red Lotus sneak up behind the gunman.

Jessica's hand moved forward and tossed the canister towards the gunman, it landed in the sand next him and within arm's reach of Red Lotus. Red Lotus picked it quickly, rose to her feet and swung the heavy object towards the visor of the gunman as she stood behind him. The impact from the blow cracked open his visor, and a loud hiss bellowed as air and heat from inside of his helmet escaped quickly, while exposing his face to the suffocating sands of the storm and the not so nice pressure of Mars atmosphere. He fell to the ground, losing his grip on his rifle, and then later his own life.

Option number three: Don't negotiate with terrorists.

"One of our pilots... I'm guessing he's the reason we're in this mess," McTavish said gazing down at the dead gunman.

"Have you found everyone else?" Jessica asked him.

"Saw Piller and Fisher over there, they told me you went to gather supplies. Came over to help, then ran into buddy around the corner."

Jessica stepped towards Red Lotus, and extended her hand out. Not a fist like the last time, rather a hand shake. "Thanks for the help," she said to her.

"Thank you for helping my team," Red Lotus said smiling.

Rescue transports arrived at their location minutes later. The death of the HLF gunman sent a message to the station above that someone on the surface suddenly flat lined. Hyperion squadron, Piller and Fisher were all picked up afterwards and ascended up towards Ares station Gamma. She was pleased with everyone's performance; McTavish taking it upon himself to find aid, Fisher staying calm even when he was close to death, Piller for staying with him to keep him alive longer. These were people Jessica would be grateful to work with again in the future. She wasn't sure if they'd have to redo the survival training excise, but if she had to do it again, she wouldn't hesitate to do it with those three.

-o-

Eddie R. Hicks is a Canadian author known as a man of many talents, and for good reason. He's educated in media arts, journalism, and culinary arts, and now he writes dark and sexy science-fiction thrillers such as the Splintered Galaxy series.

If he's not working with skilled chefs in the restaurant industry, baking an epic red velvet cake for the hell of it, or playing video games, then he's in front of his computer doing what he always dreamed of doing since he was a kid: storytelling.

Homepage: **https://eddierhicks.wordpress.com**
Mailing List: **http://eepurl.com/cuJS-L**

Pithos

by Mark Gardner

Smoke billowed from broken third story windows. Police Officers herded back onlookers. Sawhorse barriers kept the people back, but reporters and cameramen climbed over.

The three-alarm fire was a big story, not because of the potential loss of life or property damage or even the simple primal desire to see and command fire itself, but because of who the Fire Commissioner was. Danny Peterson was the youngest person to ever hold the position of Fire Commissioner in the city's history. She also happened to be a woman. Women's rights and equality were all well and good on paper and when scholars discussed and debated it in universities, but in reality, the equality portion of the debate was the most poignant. Women earned less than their male counterparts and women were still considered by many to be fragile. Many difficult jobs, including firefighting, were considered men's work. Losing a male firefighter in the line of duty was a tragedy, but to lose a woman? People just wouldn't accept it.

There are those who insist that there is equality, but even in today's age, a majority of society believes a woman's job is to maintain the household and pop out male heirs on demand. 'Barefoot and pregnant in the kitchen' was not just a tongue-in-cheek expression; it was the expectation of not only most men, but also millions of women everywhere. A woman was perfectly suited to be a schoolteacher or a waitress; even a doctor or politician, but not a combat engineer or firefighter. These beliefs were continually perpetuated by a male-dominated culture. There were scant exceptions, and any woman who strayed from these expected societal roles were branded with the scarlet 'F' of Feminism.

Danny Peterson knew she wanted to be a firefighter at a very young age. Her parents were not firefighters, nor was anyone in her extended family. She didn't live in a neighborhood where hero firefighters lived, and otherwise made their presence known. No tragedy in her past compelled her to want to fight fires. She had no reason by society's expectations to want to be a firefighter. Societal norms reflected what society thought it wanted, but society couldn't possibly factor the reasons that resulted in Danny Peterson wanting to fight fires.

The desire was planted at an early age when Danny watched a multi-part documentary on a public broadcasting station. That documentary was about the life of firefighters. During the five-day program, many firefighters candidly revealed the tremendous lack of funding to keep these unsung heroes safe. From aging equipment to poor facilities, firefighting was a dangerous occupation, but undeservedly so. So at age seven, Danny knew her life goal was to fight fires and ensure no hero had to perish due to a lack of technology or funding. While many little girls her age were worrying if their outfits matched their shoes, Danny worried about the trials and tribulations of firefighters. Danny consumed books, trade magazines, and websites focusing on firefighters and firefighting technology. She begged her parents to take her to firefighting museums.

When her interest in firefighting lore lasted five or six years, her parents started actively encouraging her interests. Not that they hadn't encouraged her in the past, but she was a little girl – and little girls were not interested in being firefighters. Firefighting and its accoutrement was the exclusive domain of little boys. She didn't outgrow her interests in firefighting, and so she started making frequent trips to visit the local volunteer fire department. She became their unofficial mascot, spending more and more time there as her parents permitted. She hated the condescending role as a mascot, but she endured for the sake of the firefighters she knew. Over time she convinced her parents to organize bake sales and junk drives to raise money for the fire department. At age thirteen, while her schoolmates were worrying about which boys liked which girls, Danny worried if she would be accepted to a junior firefighting academy. The academy seemed to be used by the local magistrate to encourage troublemakers or otherwise delinquent youths to do something useful with their lives. Many of them chose the academy to avoid juvenile detention. Danny chose it to hone her passion into a useful skill set.

Danny excelled at the academy; her life moved progressively toward college with degrees and multiple certifications in the art of firefighting. She firmly believed firefighting was not a science, but an art. When she decided to run for the elected position of Fire Commissioner at the age of twenty-two, there was quite the debate. The old arguments of gender roles were on everyone's minds. She had the backing of any firefighter who had ever met her. The old-timers from that first volunteer fire department were her most vocal supporters – having known her most of her life. The politicos did not like her at all. She fervently and loudly advocated for more funding and training for the improvement and education of firefighting. She was always interested in new technologies, technologies that were usually expensive, and often did not pan out. These politicians feared her election because she definitely had the support of the firefighters, as well as the general population. Her passion for the craft was the most cogent evidence for election.

Danny's win over the incumbent, and a field of other hopefuls, was historical. This was a city that could never seem to get any policy ratified, or person elected by any means. It seemed as though nothing ever got done. Danny's popularity was so strong she won not only the majority of the public vote, but she achieved a landslide victory that was considered by many of her supporters to be unanimous. At age twenty-two she was an elected official and had powerful sway over the voting public. The politicos feared this power, claiming it would be her downfall.

#

Danny surveyed the scene surrounding the three-alarm fire.

"Get those reporters out of my perimeter," she shouted.

Police officers immediately moved to round up errant news crews. Many of these officers were older than Danny by several, and in a few cases many, years. Despite this, they did their job efficiently; after all, she was the Fire Commissioner. Danny didn't lord over the individual fire crews or their captains. She knew many of them personally and trusted their judgment. Her presence was not really needed here, but the freshness of her election and the growing regional and national attention necessitated she be present.

The fire was rapidly contained. The fire itself wasn't the issue. The size of the building required multiple attacks to contain and suppress the flames. Containment was nearing completion; several crews were entering the building to prevent flare-ups and to continue the suppression effort. Everyone was starting to relax. Many of the units were breaking down and cleaning equipment. They started transporting equipment and personnel to their fire stations around the city.

Suddenly, the ground below the spectators rumbled. It was enough to knock many of them off their feet and set off car alarms blocks away. Danny was glad the perimeter was established in the earliest stages of the suppression effort. A BLEVE, boiling liquid expanding vapor explosion, consumed the bottom floor of the building. The BLEVE scorched vehicles and singed personnel as far away as one hundred meters. The BLEVE moved so quickly that no one had a chance to react, and it burned out quickly. There was still A-triple-F, advanced film forming foam, everywhere so the building didn't flare up again. Other than some very scared bystanders, no one appeared to be seriously injured.

A commotion from one of the crews attracted Danny's attention. Something was happening, and there were a lot of professional fire fighters upset about something. The colorful language coming from the crew chief of the unit in the building was carrying; something had gone wrong.

"I want a crew in there yesterday! Get your shit together! Let's move it! Move! Move! Move!"

Danny recognized the crew chief by the ball cap that was his attempt to conceal his receding hairline. He was supposed to be on vacation, but stopped to assist on the way out of town.

Danny ran up to the group, her duffle flopping against her hip. "Chief, what's going on?"

"Miss Peterson," he greeted.

Danny ignored the formal nature he addressed her; he had always called her Danny, but this was a stressful event.

"We think that the BLEVE was the result of the failure of a flammable liquid storage facility under this building. Our team was investigating and we believe they were securing access to the storage tanks. There hasn't been any radio contact since the explosion. We need a crew in there now!"

The chief returned to barking orders to get a proper crew together to investigate. Without hesitation Danny spoke up, "Chief, I have my gear right here, you get me three other guys, and we'll get in there."

The chief turned to make sure he had heard her correctly only to see her suiting up and adjusting the mask to her OBA, or oxygen breathing apparatus. Within seconds of agreeing to go in, Danny had a crew of three and they were running toward the building.

Getting to the basement to assess the storage tank was not any harder than many of the other scenes they witnessed during their careers as professional firefighters. They made good time to the access hatch, and began the search for the missing crew. It was sometimes difficult, and they had to stay in visual contact with each other at all times. They were eager to rescue their missing comrades but safety was paramount – losing another crew wouldn't help anyone.

They were able to locate all members of the missing crew except one. The search continued as the rescued crewmembers were evacuated to safety. It was painstakingly slow returning for each crewmember, but they were a team and forced themselves to stay together. One firefighter was still unaccounted for and Danny's crew began to worry they wouldn't find their comrade in time.

Danny scrutinized the articulated access hatch again. Something doesn't add up, she thought. There were charred uniform tatters peeking out from the seal. She grasped the latch with both hands and pulled. She hoped the hatch would give way before her back did. The hatch groaned against her efforts, but opened nearly falling on her. She scrambled out from under the path of the opening hatch, and those around began shouting for help. A burned, face down body was floating in who knew what flammable liquid. It appeared they would be recovering remains today.

#

At the hospital, Danny spent a lot of her time watching over the unconscious firefighters. Aside from the bruises and burns on some exposed skin, there were four broken ribs, a broken arm, a broken shoulder and a dislocated knee. As the firefighters regained consciousness, they pieced together the chronology of the explosion: The fallen firefighter was in the lead. He was standing inside the open hatch of the flammable liquid storage tank when he saw the ignition of the liquid. It was quicker for him to close the hatch and presumably rely on his gear to protect him from the blast. He successfully closed the hatch cutting off the oxygen, but his uniform coat had snagged on the hatch frame. He had not been fast enough and the existing oxygen mixed with the flammable vapor and exploded before the oxygen was depleted from the tank. The resulting explosion threw the surviving firefighters away from the center of the explosion. It had all happened in scant seconds from discovery to explosion. His quick thinking saved the lives of his fellow firefighters. The firefighter's name was Terry Mann. He was named after his father, some kind of physician. He had no chance of survival once he made the decision to save his brothers. Plummeting ten meters into a tank of burning liquid and exploding vapor was not a pleasant way to die.

Tears welled up in Danny's eyes and she excused herself from the room. Terrance Mann Jr. was one of the most outspoken firefighters in favor of Danny's run for Fire Commissioner. He attended all her debates and posed some of the most difficult questions. Danny didn't believe he was being malicious in what questions he asked, and answering those tough questions had solidified some of the people who were on the fence. Terry Mann was a constant presence during her candidacy, and she did not doubt he would be chief of a station soon enough. They had met frequently for coffee and talk. He maintained an aloof nature, but she suspected his façade hid a well of feelings he kept to himself. They managed to meet so frequently; she started looking forward to those future meetings. When schedules or work prevented him from meeting her, she missed him. Their relationship had moved beyond the familiar and was just starting the sparks of an impending romance.

In the hallway she attempted to gather her composure. Less than a week after assuming her duties as Commissioner, she had a fatality. Not just any fatality, but her friend. The whole situation teetered on ironic circumstance.

A nurse rushed up to Danny, "Miss Peterson! I need you to come with me immediately!"

Whatever the emergency was, it was better than thinking about Terry's last moments. The reprieve, although temporary, was a welcome distraction. She followed the nurse down a few halls and found herself in the intensive care unit. She couldn't figure out what was so important in the ICU, last she had heard the rescued firefighters had been moved. One of them had even been released, she thought.

As she rushed by groups of firefighters and well-wishers, she picked up fragments of hushed conversation. They all seemed to be talking about Terry Mann. It didn't make sense – Terry Mann died saving his team. What was so important that she was rushed to the ICU?

The head of the ICU burst out of the room they were all gathered around, "We've stabilized him and in a few hours we will be transferring him to a burn unit." He held up his hands to stem the tide of questions. "Terry is in a medically induced coma, and has third degree burns over seventy-two percent of his body. His chance of survival is less than four percent."

The eruption of questions and the thundering of news reporters invading the waiting room was lost on Danny. The three sentences the doctor spoke rattled around in her brain. Terry was alive, but for how long? She closed her eyes and tried to envision the closest burn unit with the facilities to care for her friend.

She stood, testing her legs to see if they would do as they were told. She wiped barely perceptible tears from her cheeks and rushed to the parking lot.

#

Terry Mann was transferred to the burn unit by helicopter. Danny drove straight to the burn unit. She ignored the ding and the indicator warning of a low fuel level. It was a ninety minute drive, but she made it there in seventy-five. She was one of the first to arrive, and her minor celebrity status gained her access to Terry Mann's doctors. She felt a minor pang of guilt muscling into their meeting, but she cared enough for Terry to worry about the political repercussions. Perhaps you care too much, a voice in her head chimed. She ignored the chiming voice just as she had the low fuel warning.

#

It had been five hours since the initial discovery Terry Mann was still alive, and just shy of three hours since Danny had arrived at the burn unit, when she heard a helicopter approaching. It circled the building twice and landed without anyone but her noticing. Danny was on the roof by the time it landed, but no one was rushing out to greet it, no gurneys or nurses; it was as if a helicopter did not exist.

Three men emerged from the hatch as the door slid back and recessed into the fuselage. The first figure to emerge looked oddly familiar to her, but Danny couldn't quite place him. The next occupant was in a military uniform. Some sort of Special Forces, she thought as she watched the man conduct himself. The final occupant was a nondescript short man; he must have been a lab tech or other support staff. Their importance obvious, Danny focused her attention of the first two. As the trio got closer, she continued to have flashes of recognition of the first man, but her overtaxed brain was having the worst time identifying him.

When they made their way to the elevator door Danny was standing in, the helicopter departed with the same abruptness as when it landed.

Danny overheard one of the orderlies speak to two of the men. "Colonel Bishop, Doctor Mann, please follow me."

Her flashes of recognition now made sense; Dr Mann was an older version of Terry Mann. She had never met him, but he was a dead ringer for Terry, or more precisely, Terry was a dead ringer for his father.

Danny followed the group as they walked calmly down the corridor. She fought against demanding that the elevator club hurry to her friend's side. No one stopped her from following when the trio conferred with Terry's doctors.

"Miss Peterson here has been making decisions for Terry since her arrival," the doctor informed the senior Mann. "But now you're here Doctor Mann, you'll be assuming that responsibility."

Dr Mann glanced in Danny's direction, "Thank you Miss Peterson, you're welcome to stay and be in the loop. My son has mentioned a fondness for you during your recent campaign."

Danny smiled, despite her and Terry's agreement to keep their relationship secret. "You're most welcome, if you need anything, let me know."

Dr. Mann gestured to the Special Forces soldier. "That's what Colonel Bishop is here for, but I appreciate the sentiment nonetheless."

Colonel Bishop looked in her direction, but said nothing. He was carrying a large metal suitcase, but he and the lab tech stayed in the background and did their best to stay out of the way.

The lead physician and Dr Mann were in a heated debate. "I'm not sure we should be performing any experimental procedures right now." He flung a curtain closed between them and potential eavesdroppers. "Your son is stable, but he is at risk for any number of infections. His chances for survival are too low."

"That's why we need to do this." Dr Mann jerked his thumb in the direction of the metal suitcase. "We can find out what his wishes are."

Danny felt compelled to interrupt. "How can we know what he wants?"

Dr. Mann looked to Colonel Bishop, but the Colonel stoically made no attempt to be part of the conversation.

"We have an experimental technology that allows us to switch bodies, transfer consciousness from one body to another. Joe here is volunteering to trade bodies with Terry for this procedure."

Danny stared wide-eyed at Terry's father and Joe. "You can't possibly be serious? That sounds like science fiction."

Dr Mann sighed. "Miss Peterson, the only reason you are involved at all is my son expressed a fondness for you. He believes the two of you have a future together." He stepped forward and placed a hand on the quarantine glass separating him from his son. "If you feel you are unable to control yourself, you'll have to leave. The decision has already been made. Here is a federal writ of authority authorizing his transfer to our facility if needed. I would prefer to do this here, rather than risk my son's health by relocating him, but I will if there are any disagreements here. We will start the procedure in thirty minutes."

Danny knew not to push the issue. If she wanted to stay involved, she was going to have to go along with whatever Terry's father had planned. She was able to watch the procedure from the next room through a glass window, but it was all very confusing. The device Colonel Bishop and Dr Mann were connecting to Terry and Joe the

Tech was the same dimensions of a toaster oven, with a bundle of wires and a harness with electrodes leading to both men. She was skeptical anything would come of this, but she diligently watched and waited as she was expected. If this experiment could save Terry, she would hope for the best.

#

At the allotted time, Dr Mann rotated some sort of knob on the device and flipped a switch. She expected more, but nothing seemed to happen.

Joe the lab tech screamed, "Get the fuck outta here!"

His arms and legs were flailing, pulling the electrodes off. He rolled over and off the gurney falling to the floor. He lay there unmoving. No one moved. No one spoke. Everyone was in shock.

A raspy voice came from the floor, "Where's my gear? What the fuck's goin' on? I can't move, is someone gonna help me up or what?"

Dr Mann and Colonel Bishop rushed over to help the fallen man get him into a sitting position on the gurney.

Dr Mann held the technician's floppy head in both hands. He tried to speak in soothing tones, but his eyes were welling up with tears. His voice cracked as he whispered, "Boy, I thought I lost you!"

"Dad? What are you doing here? Why can't I move?"

"Terry, you were in an accident."

"What happened? Last thing I remember was fighting to close that hatch in the warehouse. It was going to explode."

Terry reached up to grasp Dr Mann's hands and saw his own hands for the first time, "What the fuck is this? These aren't my hands!"

Dr Mann lowered his son's temporary body to the gurney, "Relax, you were injured, we had to perform an experimental procedure on you."

"The hell with relaxin', tell me what the fuck is going on!"

Dr. Mann pointed to Danny and gestured for her to come in the room. Danny ran into the room and peered at Terry, scrutinizing his face for recognition. "Terry? Is it really you? Uh... Terry, you died saving your crew from a BLEVE."

"Miss Peterson, enough with the theatrics. My son did not die, he was only seriously injured."

"Terry, they did something, and you are in someone else's body. Someone get me a mirror!" There was some shuffling and a flurry of activity while the assembled staff attempted to locate a mirror. By the time they got her a mirror, Terry was able to manipulate Joe's arms and fingers. He grasped the mirror and looked into it to see Joe's face looking back. Terry was obviously doing okay; he was sticking out his tongue and making faces at the mirror.

Dr Mann scowled at his son's frivolity, "Well it appears he is able to manipulate the host body. Okay, that's enough fun for now." Dr Mann took the mirror away, "Can you sit up and wiggle your fingers and toes?"

Terry complied and expertly moved Joe's fingers and toes.

"Now touch your thumb to each of your fingers, starting with your index finger an moving down to your pinkie." Terry found he was not able to perform this request as easily as he had dispatched the first one. His fingers felt sluggish, as if there was some kind of delay between the thought and the execution. He smirked and thought this must be what law enforcement looked for when conducting a field sobriety test.

Suddenly Terry Jr asked, "What happened to the dude whose body I am using?"

Danny pointed towards the oxygen tent, "He is occupying your body."

Terry rolled over to see his burned and mangled body, "I didn't make it out of that warehouse, did I?"

"Well you did, but it will only be temporary. You have third degree burns over seventy-two percent of your body and you are at high risk of infection. If you beat the rapidly dwindling odds, you will end up being permanently disfigured..." She trailed off, knowing he knew what was going to happen. They had both known firefighters burned less severely than he was. They ended up with permanent disfigurements. Some were also addicted to pain killers; that was no way to live.

Terry demanded, "So, how's this gonna go down?"

Dr Mann took his son's hand, "This is a combination chance to say goodbye and an experiment to see if this procedure would even work. I guess you are going to get into the history books for this one."

Danny took that opportunity to chime in, "He already is a hero to all of us, and a history book no one will ever read does not compare to his selflessness in saving everyone at that warehouse."

"Danielle Michelle Gazelle," Danny cringed at his pet name for her, "I appreciate what you are doing for me, but it isn't about glory or history books, it is about doing the right thing. This could be my last opportunity to talk to you, to tell you how I feel..."

Danny interrupted him saying, "There will be time for that later, right now you just need to focus on healing."

Suddenly the machines monitoring Terry's burned body began to sound alarms. The burned body began to spasm, and nurses and doctors rushed in. The harness and electrodes on his head were tossed aside as their training kicked in attempting to resuscitate him. Danny, Dr Mann, Terry in Joe's body and Colonel Bishop could only watch from their side of the room.

Terry was the first to speak, "What happens to me if my body dies?"

His father hesitated, "We, uh, we don't know." By now the flurry of activity around Terry's body was intensifying. The quartet of non-medical personnel was escorted out of the room to give the medical staff additional room to work.

Back in the room behind the glass window, Terry continued performing the finger dexterity test. Danny was watching him intently. He was getting pretty good at it now. It appeared the initial control issues were now fading away; he appeared to have complete control over his borrowed body. When the news of the medical staff's inability to resuscitate Terry's body reached them, they were in shock. Terry Mann was pronounced dead eleven hours after arriving at the burn unit.

#

Danny started the drive back to the city. Terry, Colonel Bishop and Dr Mann left the burn unit the same way they arrived, by unmarked helicopter. Danny was advised in the strongest language not to reveal anything she had witnessed that day. No one threatened her directly, but it was insinuated there would be quite a bit of trouble if word were to get out. She was awestruck by the events that day. The implication of her new knowledge was astounding, but she couldn't tell anyone about it.

#

Terry Mann received a hero's parade, and was buried with full honors. Danny wrote and recited a speech. It was a moving speech touting a firefighter's endless service to others and a renewed commitment toward training and education. When she concluded her speech, the gathered crowd jumped to their feet, cheering and clapping wildly.

Dr Mann, Colonel Bishop and Terry attended the funeral. Danny had a brief opportunity to see Terry before the mourners disbanded. Colonel Bishop started to speak with Danny, but the flash of a camera ended their brief encounter. Dr Mann and Colonel Bishop drew back a few paces to allow Terry and Danny a little privacy.

Terry grinned at Danny. "This is some weird mojo, huh? I liked your speech a lot. I really appreciate it."

"So what happens now? You just continue as Joe the lab tech?"

"Joe knew the risks involved, and everyone at the facility knows I am Terry and not Joe. It's basically 'business as usual.' They tested out the procedure a few more times with no glitches. It appears to work best if the hosts are unconscious for the transfer. Makes the transfer less traumatic to the senses and allows quicker motor control."

"They've tried it again?"

"Yeah. First one day, then two and three. As long as I'm alive and kickin', they'll keep trying to do it longer. I'm the first, so they haven't tried it again with me, but it looks like I will always be the longest swap. Anyway I gotta go, we had to fight to get this outing, and they are eager to have us back. I won't be able to see you again, so I wanted to say goodbye."

Terry leaned in and gave Danny a quick kiss on the lips. He was wearing the cologne she had purchased for him. A swell of emotions surged through her with that kiss, but it was brief, and the dull loneliness and sadness quickly returned.

Terry walked away. Colonel Bishop walked behind him toward Dr Mann waiting at a sedan. The trio got in; Terry paused to look at Danny once again before closing the door. The sedan drove away. As it disappeared down the driveway, Danny's eyes teared up. Many mourners mistook those tears for tears of the loss of a close colleague, but they were not. They were tears mourning a colleague's loss of freedom. She suspected Terry would never again feel free, and the world had lost a great firefighter again.

#

In the months that followed, Danny went about doing the job she was elected to do. She was expected to do a lot of politicking. She hated every minute of it, but that was how things got done. She had looked forward to her new position, but it felt empty without Terry Mann. She managed to win a few federal grants that lessened the impact of the new training programs she instituted. The Terrance Mann, Jr Memorial Fund received a large anonymous donation. She suspected it was hush money, but even if she did tell someone about Terry, no one would believe her. She operated as if Terry were gone; she knew she would never see him again. She would just have to move on, as many of Terry's friends were now doing.

Her job became commonplace. She threw herself into her work. Better to focus on the work at hand than to focus on the surreal events surrounding Terry's 'death.' Everything was running smoothly until one day about six months after her experience at the burn ward. She arrived at her office like every other morning and a familiar face smiled at her in the waiting area to her office.

"Colonel Bishop, what can I do for you?"

Bishop glanced around the room, "Can we speak privately?"

Danny motioned towards her office door, "Right this way, Colonel."

Bishop waited until Danny had closed the door before asking, "Have you seen Doctor Mann?"

"What, Recently?"

"Yes, he has been missing from our facility for about four weeks now. We believe he has gone rogue."

"Why, what happened?"

"Well, there is a flaw with the swapping process. It seems when the switch happens, the original consciousness of both bodies is suppressed, but that suppression is only temporary. By day one hundred-twenty, the host consciousness starts to regain control over the body."

"What happened to Terry?"

"Uh Miss Peterson, I don't know to tell you this, but Terry Mann developed a severe case of paranoid schizophrenia and dissociative identity disorder. None of the existing anti-psychotic drugs were able to help him. His mental state was rapidly deteriorating. Eight weeks ago he assaulted some staff members, abducted Dr Mann and was able to elude us for about two weeks."

"And you're telling me this because..."

"Because, the retrieval of Doctor Mann is a high priority. During a standoff, Terry was holding Doctor Mann hostage. Terry was shot and killed to ensure Doctor Mann's safety. A week later, Doctor Mann escaped custody with one of the early prototypes he developed. That was four weeks ago. We discovered he stockpiled a significant amount of cash. He had also stolen some equipment and parts needed to build another device. We think he blames us for his son's death. His captivity and the resulting death of his son may have been too much for him to bear. There has been intel circulating he is attempting to sell the technology to the highest bidder. Attempts to retrieve him have failed. We were able to apprehend several switched bodies and restore them, but we suspect he has financial backing from a criminal syndicate and may be able to elude us indefinitely."

Danny looked at the ceiling, "Pithos Pandora."

"Excuse me?"

Danny fixed Colonel Bishop with an icy stare, "You know, the Greek myth: Pandora's Box. Pandora was given a jar that contained all the evils of the world. She opened it against the wishes of the Greek gods, releasing evil into the world."

"I hope this nation can survive this particular kind of evil."

Danny shook her head, "When Pandora opened the jar, it wasn't just Greece that suffered, it was the entire world."

Colonel Bishop stood, touched Danny briefly on the arm, and walked out of her office. He closed her office door behind him and she never saw him or Dr Mann again.

-o-

Mark Gardner is a US Navy veteran. He lives in northern Arizona with his wife, three children and a pair of spoiled dogs. Mark holds a degree in Computer Systems and Applications, and is the Chief Operator for an Arizona radio group.

Homepage: **http://article94.com**
Mailing List: **https://article94.wordpress.com/about**

A Step on the Path

by Tom Germann

The planet was a dust ball. From orbit, it looked like a large golden ball with not a blemish in sight. It was not until they left the ship and were heading down by shuttle that they saw all the imperfections that marred that golden ball.

One of them had called it a military pleasure palace and theorized that there would be bars and brothels everywhere. The common soldiers would have their bars and the officers would have a much higher class of establishment. Some of the others had wondered what sort of kink they could find in those establishments and were sure that they could teach the 'ladies' working there a thing or two.

Yet on the flight down, they saw the blemishes and the crude laughter and roughhousing that most of them had participated in became forced. Then as they passed over the planet with the shuttles bleeding off more speed in the atmosphere they could see the endless miles of nothing. Rocks and sand. The laughter died.

The shuttles rose up over a ridge and ahead was the terraforming station. There were a number of these massive installations on any planet deemed worthy. Carefully sited and placed with a thirty year supply of fuel for the generators, they are left running while humanity carries on with more interesting things.

One young rake cheerfully informed everyone that they had been running for more than ten years now. The atmosphere from the ponds around it had increased to the point where a human could go outside without a rebreather. In ten more years there would be basic life on the planet. Building blocks for the more advanced forms to come. Within fifteen they would be releasing the low-level herbivores and then the first humans would be showing up to start building.

Everyone sneered down their noses at the young know it all. After all, if he was so smart he would have told them before they had gotten their hopes up for booze and brothels.

They carried out the worst punishment possible on the young fool.

They ignored him.

#

I understand how this group works, I always have. I recognize what they are doing and how they are going to act. If I want I could put the skin on and fit right in with them. Not just be one of them, but be one of the most popular. I know how they think and what their instincts will make them do.

They are stupid and I cannot work with them. I was not sent here to die. I was sent here to learn and become more than I was. To fulfill the requirements of my honour, my elders, my family and The Empire. All of those things are the same to me. I must win.

I sidle over to the young man who has moved to the far side of the shuttle and is enjoying the view of endless sand and rock. The sun here is brighter than on Earth or any other established colony. The air is thinner here and will be for fifty years at least. The rich will rush to claim huge swathes of land and establish the feudal system and then in a hundred years if the pollution gets out of control they will leave behind the weakest members of the family and move on to the next ready-made Garden of Eden.

This young man does not understand the mighty snub that the rest of the pack have just dealt him. Or he does not care. He may be worthy.

He looks up at me with a small smile. "Oh I'm sorry, do you want this seat for the view?"

There are rows of empty seats on this side of the shuttle. I can't make assumptions but I have to go with the odds. He is what he appears to be. A socially unaccepted individual likely from a smaller poorer house.

"No, thank you. There are several more on this side. I was actually curious about you. We weren't provided any information on the flight out and no access to media readers other than ones people brought. Yet you seemed to know a great deal about the terraforming process. Are you a spy? If you are, showing off was probably a mistake."

He grins at me. "No, good sir. I am simply the worst thing that a family can have. A historian and someone actually interested in how things work."

He says a few more things but they are useless small talk. He is right though. A fair number of the nobility don't worry about anything unless they can drink it, inject it or get a leg over it. At least until they get older and the rest of the family puts them to work on real concerns.

"So you just studied this before coming here? How did you know though?"

His smile is a bit darker. "I asked what the place would be like and pulled in some minor markers owed my family. Most of our guards and arms men are ex-military."

Something caught me. "How did you have the time to ask? Everyone was grabbed from whatever dark corner they were in at the moment and knocked out. I thought everyone woke up on the ship and the crew wouldn't talk to us." They wouldn't talk. The few dozen we saw were highly trained and skilled operatives that could easily kill and the one attempt to ambush and beat one up hadn't gone well for those who had a hand in it. All twelve were in the infirmary with broken bones, and even with quick heal, the last of them had only come out two days ago. The operatives had acted with remarkable restraint and not just killed everyone.

His answer shocks me. "I asked my family to let me go on this. I heard through some of our men about this training program and if I pass then I am in."

This boy is small, scrawny and his ship suit barely fits him. He looks like one of those gawky dogs that don't quite fit its paws or skin and you always feel sorry for. I can see bruises on him now. He was an obvious target for the pack. He must be lonely or he wouldn't have given away so much.

"In? In on what? If you know what's going on here then tell me."

He nods. "Okay. This is a special officer training program. The fast track for future leaders in the military and also for the nobility. They dump a bunch of third or fourth tier males in the line of succession. No one cares for them but the family can use them. Pass and you can get in on better activities than hoping the family marries you off to someone to lock in a contract. Government contracts, research work or other things that normally we would be blocked from. My family agreed to it, but as you can see, I'm kind of small, so the family arms men took a few days to train me. They tried but I'm not very good. But that doesn't matter. This is a leadership course. There shouldn't be any combat, just really hard course load and physical abuse. If I toe the line, get good grades and try, I should pass. I don't need to be first. Just good enough to get that mark and then I'm off to research. I prefer military with weapons, as it is what I studied up on."

I just stare at him. He volunteered?

"Why didn't your family just put your name into some of the better universities or research centres? It's not hard to get in there if you have the brains, and you have more than this entire pack does."

His smirk as I nodded at the other thirty-six nobles on the shuttle is endearing. I find myself liking him even more. I shouldn't, as that is a weakness, but he is a better person than most of the rest of the mob.

The shuttle comes around and I heave myself into the seat next to him. We are coming in too fast for a normal shuttle. But this is a military shuttle and they are actually doing a combat landing.

The red warning lights go on overhead and everyone else throws themselves into seats. Most get clipped in, some don't, and that leads to strains and sprains when we hammer into the ground and stop almost immediately. One goes flying down the aisle and hits the far door with a groan.

A voice comes over the system. "Doors opening in thirty. Head straight back and do not touch the shuttle or you'll burn." Then it clicks off.

Seconds later the rear hatch buzzes and then slowly lowers. The two of us are up and out of the seats and moving straight out away from the shuttle in a straight line. A utility vehicle has pulled up with four men in it. All are armed and there is some sort of support weapon mounted on top of it.

The small geeky character smiles as we walk forward. He speaks out of the side of his mouth.

"I never introduced myself. Reginald Osker the Fourth. Everyone calls me Reggie."

Keeping my eye on the utility vehicle which we are getting closer toward, I answer the same way. "Norbert Elantra. Call me Timer."

There is no more time to talk as we come up to the vehicle. The others join us.

A single man steps out of the vehicle. He is wearing standard fatigues with a chest rig loaded with pouches. His weapon is last generation though and it's a projectile type, not the laser that everyone is familiar with from the vids. His hat is wide brimmed and there are no rank or unit markings anywhere on his gear that I can see.

He points off to the side.

"Next shuttle is due in two minutes. Move over there and put on one of the web belts. Each one has a full water canteen. There is also a selection of hats that we recommend you put on as the air is thin and you will burn fast out here.

Reggie and I walk over and start rooting through the gear looking for what will fit us. They are one size fit all and I gratefully put the hat on my head. Just seconds in the sun and I could feel the burn.

Everyone else has joined us and the whine of engines grows to a roar while the rear hatch on the shuttle closes. It rockets down the runway and is airborne in seconds heading away from us.

The people at the vehicle didn't say anything, but looked hostile, so the pack of noble brats descended on the belts, canteens, and hats.

There was a great deal of complaining about the poor quality and how the water in the canteens was brackish and tasted odd.

The pack had isolated Reggie and me now. None were confident enough to start something with us though. Not yet anyway.

A distant roaring sound was building. There in the distance was a blur moving toward us. You could almost see the glow of the heat as the shuttle came in hard and fast.

The shriek of the airbrakes deploying wasn't kept out by hands over the ears either. It was a piercing pain. Then the shuttle was down and nozzles popped out of the ground, spraying foam onto the shuttle. It had felt like we were standing by an open oven when it had first stopped. But the foam seemed to absorb that heat and was already breaking down. The hatch opened and another horde of young nobles came trooping out.

One of them stopped, turned, walked back to the shuttle and then reached up to touch the hull.

Beside me Reggie sucked in his breath as the fool did so. The screaming started immediately and then he fell. A few of the others went over to see what was going on, and then most left him lying there screaming except for two who dragged him away and then helped him to his feet.

Whatever had happened the screams died to a deep sobbing and then everyone was with us grabbing belts. No one knew or cared what happened to him, they just didn't want to be associated with him.

"Line up! One single line facing the vehicle."

It was the same man that had directed us to the stack of gear in the first place.

Reggie and I moved to where he was pointing and stood there watching the vehicle. The rest of the crowd just stood there defiant in the face of direction from a prole. We all stood there for five, ten, fifteen minutes. The sun was just beating down on us. The sweat evaporated off of me faster than it was coming out. I had done a quick count and there had been more canteens than people so I had made sure to grab myself a spare and handed another one to Reggie. We split one canteen worth in that time.

The men in the vehicle had shade and I could see them drinking regularly.

There was no movement and the soldiers didn't seem to care. Finally, the rest of the crowd took the hint and first a few wandered over joining the line, then more, until the last one was finally moving. Most had expressed displeasure in one way or the other.

The soldiers ignored all the posturing and comments.

No one actually had the fortitude to walk up to the vehicle and demand answers. The soldiers did not look like they would truly appreciate how important these people were and that just wouldn't do. The thought of being roughly manhandled by commoners would make most of them shudder in revulsion.

When the sobbing one had joined the line holding his arms in close to his chest, one of the men in the vehicle got out and moved forward and to the side.

Like the others, he had a rifle slung at his side, a sidearm on his belt and was wearing no rank or other insignia on his uniform. When he stopped moving, he looked more like a hunting cat that I had seen in the wilds on a hunt years ago. Resting and looking half asleep the creature had moved like lightning and come out of the tree and onto one of the herd animals that had been at a watering hole we hadn't seen. We had only heard the screams for a second and then it was over.

That was what this man reminded me of. He didn't look big or intimidating. He was a jungle cat looking for the next thing to kill.

"I am the commandant of this temporary school. You will call me Sir at all times. Everyone else you will address as Staff. You will not question orders. Most of you will fail this course."

He paused and smiled grimly.

"That was your pep talk and the rules. Here is what you need to know. Be aware the rest of the candidates arrived earlier and I did not have to tell them anything. They already know what to do. You, on the other hand, are young, simpering, inbred, stupid wastes of time and space. Yet the General who I respect and whose orders I follow has directed me to train you to be leaders. Let me make something clear now so you understand. You all disgust me. Every one of you is useless and has spent time wasting resources that would have been better put to use on worthy members of the Commonwealth. Our enemies are many and waiting for us to slip and fall. You should be executed publicly to better motivate those who would have a chance with the proper motivation. Understand. Your own families sent you here knowing that the odds of you surviving are approximately one in seven. They don't care about you so don't hold out hope that they will come out here to do anything for you. This is the one warning I am going to give you."

One of the pack leaders was going to try it. He stepped forward with hands on hips and I knew the best sneer on his face that he could muster.

"Now see here! That man over there is injured and will need medical assistance. The rest of us are going to need a vehicle to get to the camp and then proper equipment for this place. I don't know who you think everyone else is but while my clan is small they fill a very important..."

The crack of the shot was incredibly loud. Much louder than the screams of the people around him that had been sprayed with bone and brain matter as the loudmouth was blown backward.

The Commandant brought the sidearm down and holstered it.

I could see the sneer on his face as he looked around at us then turned and walked back to the vehicle.

Before he climbed back in he looked at us and called out. "Welcome to Ranger Officer training. You have thirty minutes to make it inside the walls of the camp, then the gates are closed and sealed and you are on your own."

The vehicle drove off toward the distant camp and I looked around. Everyone was standing around staring at the headless body pumping blood out onto the sand. It was absorbed almost immediately. I turned and grabbed a stunned looking Reggie and started walking and dragging him with me toward the distant walled camp. It wasn't more than two klicks but better safe than sorry.

Reggie was a dead weight for the first few steps and I was about to let him go as I couldn't drag him the whole way. Then he was walking with me and mumbling.

"No no. This is wrong. Why is this happening?"

I looked over at him. Even the hat was too big for him and under it, he had gone bone white and his eyes looked like they had sunk back into his skull.

"Reggie, come on keep walking. You knew what you were getting yourself into. You told me you volunteered. You must have seen executions before?"

His mouth was opening and closing and then he seemed to get a grip on himself. He even stepped his pace out a bit so that we were walking at a reasonable clip.

"I did volunteer. I was told by my family that they had enrolled me into an army or possibly marine training program. The guards all agreed with that too. This is Ranger training. I'm going to die."

I stopped. We hadn't moved that far but no one else was moving. They were staying away from the body and ignoring the guy with the burned hand who had collapsed to the ground. Reggie looked even worse.

"So it's Ranger training for leaders and … ?"

He shook his head. "Don't you know anything about the Rangers? They're the pointed poisoned end of the stick that is used to jab at enemies of the Commonwealth. Sabotage, murder, destruction of enemy ships at anchor. Those are the guys that are sent in. They don't go in as an army, there would be maybe eight of them and they have a very high success rate for their missions. They also have a high mortality rate at eighty percent dying before they finish their tour. The Commandant shot that guy and there will be no repercussions. They can do whatever they want."

I knew all this and now I was seeing what had panicked him. Ranger training at any level wasn't about trying hard and getting through it. Ranger training was about surviving. This would be advanced training for the leadership cadre.

I shrugged and grabbed his arm again.

"Doesn't matter, Reggie. You're here now and you can't leave. So focus on making it." We walked on toward the gate.

Reggie looked back at the slow trickle of people starting to follow us.

"Shouldn't we bring the guy along who burned himself?"

I shook my head no and kept my eyes on the compound ahead. The vehicle was driving in now. Those walls had to be almost five metres high.

"Didn't you catch that briefing? The strong who are smart will survive. We were told to walk away from the shuttle and not touch anything. That foam absorbs the heat and dissolves, dissipating the heat at the same time. That fool touched the metal. He must have burns that would require an emergency room and special training. I bet those are flash burns and he is going into full shock now. He'll be dead soon. We need to focus on anyone that can help us stay alive."

Reggie stared at me. I could feel his eyes on me but he kept walking on with me toward the camp.

None of us had watches. The few with implants reported that they weren't working but it didn't matter, we were always made aware of what time it was.

Half an hour after the Commandant had briefed us, the gates to the compound closed. The burned guy never made it, just lying there in the sand sobbing.

There were staff inside that quickly organized us into groups of ten. Then we were issued kit and sleeping habs.

The entire camp had been created in a day using mining machinery which gathered sand and superheated it till it bonded together. Gaps were left for power lines and lighting to be run. There was no running water and we used something called cat scratch sanitation. Pits were dug deep into the ground and small huts were built over them. The staff told us that after we were done here the military would use this for a big exercise they had planned then it would be leveled.

We ate out of ration packs in a mess hall that had hard tables and benches that had been poured in place. Sand seemed to get everywhere and drove me slowly insane but at least I was alive. So was Reggie but I didn't think he would last for long.

We could drink all the water that we wanted. That was the first thing we were told. Dehydration would kill a man faster than you would believe possible. Yet we were not allowed to have water showers.

There were twenty-two other candidates here. They were all Rangers that had been slotted in for leadership training. They didn't talk to us until we had moved into our habitation buildings. One of them had come over, a tough looking man with tattoos and scars over most of his body. He simply walked up to the biggest group of us and made his announcement.

"I've been sent as a spokesman for the rest of my brothers as I have some patience and won't just snap some of your necks. We don't know you and we don't want to. Do not come near us or try to drag us down to your pathetic level or we will kill you. If you get any of us killed then every other brother is going to come after you until you are dead." When he panned his eyes over us they were not predatory at all. It was like looking at death's own face. "Someone nod   that   you   understand." Next to me, Reggie nodded aggressively. Scar face held his eyes for a second, nodded and walked away.

The first few days were strange.

The staff was knowledgeable and professional. They were top members of the military and it showed. Until you screwed up and then another side of them came out.

The first two weeks were basic recruit training for everyone including the rangers.

A fair number of nobles sent their kids off to military academies to instill a proper sense of duty. Really it was just boarding school with uniforms. They had a harder time because there was nothing to spit shine or big parades to organize.

I didn't go near the rangers but watched what they did and copied them. They were terrible garrison soldiers but they got the job done and they were in good shape. Uniforms were worn one day and then hung to air out for two days.

Some of our guys didn't get that and wore their uniform for a few days straight. It started falling apart by the fourth day and it earned the guy who did that the nickname of Stinky from the staff, and a beating as well.

The one staff member had a boot on Stinky's chest and was yelling in his face. "This is the gear that the army is issued. Don't like how it falls apart in a few days? Take it up with your families for providing cheap junk to the military for top dollar!"

The training was hard. Harder for Reggie as he was small and had never really exercised.

We were up every day at 0400 and then we ran and did other strength building exercises. Marching, more exercise in uniform as a group. Then we learned more foot drill and how to live in the field by setting up tents and then establishing a routine. We sat through lessons on military history and then moved to learning how to use weapons. We handled training dummies of the latest laser rifles and pistols. Then there were ballistic weapons. We spent days on the ranges set up outside of the camp firing in the heat. We weren't done until the late hours of the night when it had gotten dark. Then we would finally be allowed to collapse into bunks for a few hours' sleep before we were up the next day.

Our graduation night was bizarre as we were let off two hours early and allowed to celebrate. Everyone just collapsed in their bunks.

Reggie had made it even though it was tricky for a while. He wanted to be effective, but he was smaller and weaker, having never played a lot of sports. He tried though, and he made it.

The following two weeks were supposed to be ranger training. But before that started we had a down day.

Everyone had been in the infirmary at least once. Usually with a broken bone. A shot of quick heal and a mobile cast and then it was back out to training.

We were given a series of immunization shots and then told to go lie down as our bodies would demand sleep after this.

We obeyed.

I was lying on my bunk and Reggie was talking about what we were doing the next day and then I was gone. There was a flash of light and I was looking at people who were walking by me. They were all dead.

There was a long line of people with the last few dozen lacking a head. Then the body with no head from when we landed. The idiot who had touched the shuttle, his skin was desiccated and he stopped and eyed the canteen at my hip longingly. I ignored him and he walked on. The one who had hung himself from the light the first week when he snapped, his head was set off on an angle. The two who had lost it on the ranges and been shot down when they turned and shot a staff member. The final one was the idiot who had mocked a Ranger's mother. He walked by me but couldn't see me because his head was facing backward.

From what I had heard, I expected there to be a lot more of the nobles dead by this point.

I woke up.

We had lost a day but there didn't seem to be any rush to catch that time up. Time didn't seem to exist in this world. It was just a tool that the Staff used to tell us when to do something.

We spent two more weeks learning to become rangers. This didn't mean any of the specialized deep space or star ship training. We learned the basics. First aid, specialized weapons, armoured vehicles, survival in all conditions including extreme environmental conditions.

We deployed to the polar caps for three days. The temperature difference wasn't that bad. We were at thirty-five degrees Celsius and then we were dropped into sub-zero conditions. In the same clothing. We burrowed into the snow in a group and huddled in with everyone else that you could get close to.

Three didn't make it back from that.

We lost four more on the explosives range. They were setting up a booby trap and then the one got up and started walking away. Probably upset at some comment that offended his aristocratic airs. The charge detonated and they were all dead.

The one that had been walking away had been partially shielded and not right at the blast area so his arm was blown off and he had holes in his chest.

One of the staff shot him after a few seconds of his screaming.

Even though we had been through this training for almost three weeks the aristocratic training of the nobles just couldn't be turned off.

Everyone was bulking up, even Reggie. I had figured out that something was being put in our food or water. Likely nannites and other products to develop muscle mass.

I noticed that everyone else's aggression was increasing as well. Again, something in the food.

It was easier to do the long runs and strength training. But it was getting harder to think clearly at times especially when I was angry.

When we returned from the polar cap we had the afternoon to carry out simple training and then we were all sent to bed early.

The next morning was specialized weapon training. We started with historical weapons. Swords were easy and the few members that had been taught fencing and seemed to know what they were doing were taking everyone else through it.

We had started doing training with the other Rangers and they came over to work with us. Henri was running us through sword fighting and one of the Rangers walked over and pulled a sword from the rack and nodded at him.

"You and me now."

Henri had shrugged and taken a weapon, moved in, and they had fenced back and forth. Henri was obviously the better fencer and started toying with the ranger.

He finally lunged in and tapped his sword arm. Stepping back with a flourish and yelled. "Point!"

The ranger had shrugged, switched hands on the sword and stepped forward slicing at Henri's throat. Henri had been able to get the sword up but it had been smashed out of the way. Some of the force of the blow had been spent and these were training swords so the blade was not very sharp. But Henri's eyes bulged out and he flailed around with the sword as his throat looked like it had been crushed. Again the ranger struck and it was like watching a man with an axe hacking at a tree.

Henri crashed to the ground and the Ranger stepped forward and stomped on his throat with a booted foot.

He dropped the sword and looked around at us. "He scored the point. I survived. This isn't some sort of gym where you are trying to score. This is the real world and things want to kill you."

He turned and walked off.

Another staff member came up and we kept training.

We moved on to modern close quarters combat weapons. Maces that had power cells in the shaft. When you struck your target it would release a massive charge that could overwhelm suit systems and fry an unprotected person immediately. We only used cells on a trickle charge so that when we were hit it hurt and it hurt a lot but it didn't kill us.

We lost two more during that close quarter training but I don't know what happened. I was off with my group training and there were two more bodies dumped to the side.

The Rangers were similar to the nobles because neither cared about the other and we were all used to seeing executions while the Rangers had likely carried out a large number of executions, or perhaps just plain old killings.

The next few days passed uneventfully. Broken bones were rapidly healed and we were pushed back into training.

It felt like we had been there for months not just a few short weeks.

Then the blow up happened.

There were times when it was almost impossible to control my temper and small fights were happening regularly. The staff just treated it as normal and let us work through it. Usually with a black eye or perhaps a broken bone if the two had a real issue with each other.

The cliques had broken down. They still existed but now they were smaller and nastier. The groups had broken down along some strange lines but the meanest was the one that was most threatening.

There were no names, just eight aristocratic brats that had been raised in military academies and they were all smart and had extensive training in different martial skills. They were a real threat and the only group that was able to mostly hold its own against others in training.

They were strong, smart and mean. Whatever had been put in the food increased that. A lot. None of their group had really screwed up either.

They decided it would be fun at the end of Ranger training to send one of their muscle at Reggie. They wouldn't bother me as I was a nobody. One smaller group had tried it out with me earlier and I had broken the arms of two of them. I was left alone after that.

Reggie had filled out and was doing okay for most of the training. He was the smartest one there and willing to help. But that just made him look weak.

At dinner, he was walking to the far corner where I was already sitting shoveling the glop in my mouth when a hulking bruiser stuck his foot out and tripped him.

Reggie was small but fast. He caught himself on their table and kept walking to the snickers behind him.

He was almost fast enough to dodge the blow that caught him from the side. The bruiser had swung from sitting. Grazed, Reggie was knocked over and flew into the next table over with a thud and collapsed.

This was a standard tactic. Fake incident and then a beating for whoever was chosen. The bruiser got up.

"Little scum. You come along here thinking you're better than us and start fondling our table? Apologize you rutting little piglet."

He moved forward and was getting ready to kick Reggie, who was lying there. He must have been hit harder than I had seen.

The ration bag hit him in the face and exploded with warm gravy and chunks of soy meat everywhere, causing him to scream. I grabbed Reggie and pulled him out of the way as the bruiser screamed and kicked out before he fell over, clawing at his eyes.

The other seven at the table stood up and they were ready to fight us with murder in their eyes. Then there was the sound of clapping from the door. Two of the rangers were standing there watching events unfold and the same one that had lectured us the first day was clapping.

"Hey girls, looks like you need some real men to dance with. We've got some time. You wanna party with us?"

The seven hesitated and then slumped back onto their benches. The two rangers smiled and walked out. The rage in the air had blown out but the look the seven were giving us let me know this wasn't over.

We spent four more weeks there training. We moved out to deep space for an accelerated course of operations in vacuum, which left me and everyone else with nightmares. We carried out assault landings in shuttles and drop pods.

There was another planet in-system that was much further along in the terraforming process. We were there for a good bit of our training.

I will have nightmares until the day I die of the things that happened.

By the last day of training we had lost another nine of my fellow nobles.

Then we were released in the camp. Standing there filthy, covered with bites and lesions from our time in the field, finding it difficult to breathe through lungs that were struggling with the thinner air after being on a different world and adjusting to a higher oxygen content.

For the second time, we saw the Commandant. He walked out and looked at all of us. Those that were left anyway.

All twenty-two rangers were there. But we had gone from seventy-eight to forty-eight. Even now most of us were still hard-bitten nobles that refused to accept anything other than our due.

The Commandant just smiled in a crooked manner.

"Graduation day is tomorrow. The water restriction is lifted and you may all shower and clean up tonight. After that, the drinking mess will be open but be careful not to drink too much as you need to be presentable for the ceremony tomorrow. Dismissed."

The Rangers turned and walked away to their own quarters. We all turned and ran for ours. A shower. A real water shower.

#

I had taken my time and gone through the shower last, as had Reggie. I savored the cold water that sprayed on me. As soon as we stepped out of the sealed building I felt the ever present sand and grit working its way back into my clothes.

It didn't matter.

I started heading for the mess where squeeze bulbs of alcohol were being handed out as if it was a party back home.

Reggie's hand on my shoulder stopped me. "You know that with a much thinner atmosphere and no one having had a proper meal for weeks any alcohol will flatten us, right? I don't think we're done and this is something else to screw us over."

I paused. He was right. But we had to go or the good times would turn bad and then all that suppressed rage would come out. On us, the outsiders.

"No. We have to go in. Just sip your drink and dump most of it out on the ground when we wander outside. 'Drink' as much as everyone else."

We went into the party. The night was long and I dismissed my worries as I could do nothing with them.

#

The staff had roused us none too gently the next morning and had us outside in our basic kit formed up in four ranks. Reggie and I pretended to be as drunk as anyone else but it wasn't easy.

The Commandant came over smiling. The rest of the Rangers weren't there though for some reason. They were sitting up high on the bleachers looking relaxed.

"Gentlemen, I want to thank you all for participating in this training. Soon you will be heading back off world to your families and positions that they have arranged for you." He paused.

I knew that half of the nobles would barely be able to wait to be on the ship before they would be drafting statements on the death and outright murder of so many of their own. The other half would do it on board ship as it was heading out system.

"But there is a problem. You see when we run a Ranger training course like this, there are numbers games that are played. We have too many passes right now. So what is going to happen is you are going to pair off in the pit and fight. Winner passes. Loser doesn't."

I went cold. There were armed staff up on the walls watching and we had no choice but to move to the ring. I would be okay but what about Reggie?

The first two names were called and in they went. The fight was awkward because they were both too drunk but eventually one of them was on the other's back, pushing his opponents face deep into the sand while screaming and vomiting.

It went on like that. Then someone called Reggie and the Bruiser's name. That big guy had looked rough but had become very sober as people died in the ring.

It was a fast fight. Reggie got a few hits in but it did nothing to the bruiser. Then Reggie was being clinched and he screamed as his shoulder popped. He fell.

There was nothing I could do.

The bruiser moved in but Reggie's booted foot smashed into his knee and there was a crack. Bruiser was screaming. Reggie kicked him in the crotch from the ground and that damn fool was shrieking.

Reggie kicked him mostly to death and then standing over him grabbed his head and with a scream twisted. We all heard the crack.

"I apologize, *piglet*." He spat on the corpse and walked out of the ring.

I was next.

I had to make this good and stand out. The Commandant knew who I was. So did the Rangers. I had been guided and now they needed to see the quality of what they had molded.

I fought the leader of the eight. He was tough. In his own eyes.

He came in hard and fast hoping to get close and cripple me.

I grabbed his right wrist and broke it, then the elbow. I smashed his left leg at the knee and again there was a crack and I could feel it splinter.

He fell screaming to the sand and I took him apart. The left arm was next and then his right leg.

He was still screaming and blubbering. I grabbed his shattered arm and pulled him onto his stomach. He couldn't resist. Then I put my foot on the back of his head and pushed his face into the sand grinding it in. It took a little while for him to drown in the sand but it was worthwhile.

I am like my Grandfather and Father. I cannot stand those who would take advantage of their position, and finally I could let my anger out.

The last fights finished and we were formed up into two ranks to march out to the shuttle. Some of the staff came out and dragged the bodies off to recyc where they would be broken down into their constituent elements to then be put to good use building a planet.

I realized something. Happy eighteenth birthday Sir Elantra of the Order.

#

The Commandant smiled at us as we lined up to head over to the shuttle.

"Again, thank you, gentlemen, for participating. I know some of you would like to report what happened to the Commonwealth. Please feel free. Every second of the ring there was recorded as you murdered a fellow noble. The sentence for that is automatically death, with no appeal. Good-bye."

He turned and left while we walked to the shuttle. Reggie walked with a smile. He would be a scientist now.

Me? I was heading home and Grandfather would be proud. I would be the next ruler of our world as the first son. Baron of Karel IV.

This had been the final test. Survive and move on or fail and die. Now my Grandfather would look at me and I could finally be the officer he wanted.

-o-

A father, a reservist and more, Tom loves science fiction. Writing and reading it creates gateways to new worlds of imagination. While still relatively new to writing these stories out, he has been creating entertaining stories for years. Be aware that there are often twists and turns in his stories and they do not always follow the traditional models.

Homepage: **http://www.tgermann-sf-guy.com**
Mailing List: **http://eepurl.com/bYnxvD**

Rituals

by Rick Partlow

"The end move in politics is always to pick up a gun" - R.
Buckminster Fuller.

McKay was pushed into his acceleration couch as the lander
rocketed away from her monolithic mothership, leaping with a
lemming's enthusiasm toward the sullen planet below.

It's just another Balls-In, he repeated silently, just another
simulation. That was what he'd told himself on every Ballistic
Insertion he'd experienced since he'd enlisted. It had worked, too,
back when he'd been a private, green and fresh out of college. But
now he was Second Lieutenant Jason McKay, commanding his own
reaction squad, and that blue-green hemisphere that filled the
forward viewscreens wasn't Earth. He was some twenty light-years
from home, above the second world out from 82 Eridani, and it was
all too real.

Whatever could have possessed me, he wondered, to go to
Officer's Candidate School?

"Sir?" Sergeant Wolczk turned to him, confusion furling his Cro-
Magnonesque brows. McKay realized with a start that he must have

unconsciously vocalized part of that internal question.

"Uh...I was just asking if everything was secure, Gunny," McKay lied.

"Oh, yes, sir," the burly Marine sergeant said with a grin. "All the troops're strapped in and everything's battened down."

"Good. You okay back there, Constable Khải?" McKay craned his neck around to speak to the man behind him. Looking lost in the smallest combat armor they'd been able to find, Phan Văn Khải made an unlikely cop; but the spindly, fiftyish Laotian was the chief constable of Inferno, one of the roughest colony worlds of the Republic.

"Yes, I am quite secure, thank you," Khải replied.

"When the guano hits the turbines, stick close to me," McKay told him. "Don't get me wrong," he hastened to add, "I'm sure you can handle yourself, but Marines train to a certain attack pattern, and if you're not in a 'friendly' zone, they're likely to pump you first and ID the remains later."

"I will do as you suggest, Lieutenant. Thank you for your concern."

"It'd be a good idea for you to watch where you're moving too, Captain," McKay told the other occupant of the command compartment who sat beside, and dwarfed by comparison, Constable Khải. Captain Miguel Hernandez was a fair-haired Titan in the bulky, black armor of the Colonial Guard, a weighty rocket rifle wedged between his knees.

"I will go where I damn well please, McKay!" the Argentinian snapped. "And I still plan to file an official protest with the governor about this unacceptable command structure. I am your superior officer, and I should be leading this attack."

"Regulations, Captain," McKay reminded him, visibly unimpressed with the man. "Only a Marine officer can lead Marines in a combat situation."

"Then it should be Guard troops leading the assault!" The big man smacked the plastic lining on the bulkhead with his armor-gloved fist.

"Nearest Guard troops are two days out, on Eden," McKay said, a flush of heat travelling swiftly up the back of his neck. "It's only blind luck we were this close to Inferno. I assume you'd like to retake the base while some of your soldiers are still alive?"

The Captain's eyes narrowed in a look meant to seem threatening, but rendered ludicrous by the convergence of the man's bushy blond eyebrows. "I find your tone offensive, Lieutenant."

"That's a damn shame," McKay grunted, feeling the checks slip off his temper. He was millimeters from a court-martial offense when the lander's deorbit burn ended and free-fall rescued him. "If you'll excuse me, I'm going to brief my squad."

Unstrapping himself, McKay grabbed a handhold and shoved himself through the hatchway back into the troop compartment. Sergeant Wolczk scrambled to follow, moving in the null gravity with practiced ease.

"Ten-shut!" Wolczk's voice cut through the squad's chatter as the pair halted themselves inside the compartment.

The squad fell silent and turned in their acceleration couches to face McKay. He silently scanned the faces of the nine men and three women. Remembering their names wasn't too difficult: they were emblazoned on the breasts of their fatigues. What was hard was attaching anything meaningful to those names. Out of the twelve, he could only put together as much as a thumbnail sketch of three.

Closest to him was Corporal Ari Shamir, the quiet young Israeli who always seemed to be reading something. Next to the corporal was Shawn Dobbs, a giant of a man who McKay knew didn't give a damn for officers in general and him in particular. Over in the corner was Joanna Corson, the skinny, Canadian private with the squeaky voice that everyone was always mimicking. He'd only been in command for four months, and almost half of that had been spent unconscious in the g-tanks. He wished he knew them better... but it was probably better that he didn't.

"It's about a half-hour till we hit atmosphere," McKay announced in what he hoped was a calm, steady voice. "You know the score. Some local politician name'a Ngô Bảo Châu has the Asian immigrants in New Saigon stirred up about the local conditions. He's got about a hundred of them together, mostly PanAsian Alliance exiles from the Uprising, and they took Inferno's Colonial Guard armory, got ahold of some heavy weapons. The local cops only have antipersonnel, riot-control stuff, so they called on us to pull the CeeGee's ass out of the fire."

"So what else is new?" somebody muttered, *sotto voce.*

"What kinds of heavy weapons are we talking about, sir?" Shamir asked.

"Rocket rifles, assault cannons, lots of heavy personal armor,"

McKay replied. "Maybe a couple of attack vehicles. Châu and his people have combat experience, but we don't know if they're familiar with high-tech targeting systems. Standard tactics, though: hit 'em hard and fast, and hit 'em again before they know what's happening. Take out their vehicles first, then penetrate the building. I wish we could just level the place, but we've got to bust out the Guard troops they're holding."

"How'd they take the armory in the first place?" asked a skinny private with ears two sizes too big for his head. His name was... Nichols, that was it.

"Inside help: civilians working maintenance. They suckered everyone in, gassed them with their own security system. The good Captain managed to escape to warn the cops and they called us...we were the closest thing available since the *Bradley* was refueling at the solar antimatter factory. Khải and Hernandez managed to get to the planet's only shuttle and came up to help us coordinate the attack."

"Damn CeeGee's were always a bunch of amateurs," Dobbs muttered.

"At ease with that crap, Dobbs!" Wolczk snapped.

"Just stay tight and listen to Gunny and we'll all get through this," McKay finished, hoping he sounded convincing to them, because he sure as hell didn't believe it himself.

#

Wind buffeted the bulbous lander as it descended through the upper layers of Inferno's atmosphere, the ship's delta wings grabbing furtively at the gradually thickening air, its heat shielding glowing with ionized fire. This was the part of a Balls-In that always made McKay sweat: the moment between the shutdown of the hydrogen-fluorine rockets and the start-up of the ramjets.

The jets won't start! his mind screamed at him. *We're all going to die!*

But the crew in the cockpit was expert; the jets sucked in air and ignited, kicking them all soundly in the pants. McKay resumed breathing and hit the intercom switch on the bulkhead beside him.

"All right, boys and girls," he announced, "we de-ass in twelve minutes. Wait for the smoke and use your thermal sights. Everyone secure helmets and check your seals. Good luck and good hunting."

"Good hunting?" Khải repeated, cocking an eyebrow.

"Just a kind of ritual." McKay shrugged uncomfortably, not wanting to go into how he had picked up the expression from a previous commander. He slipped on his armored battle helmet and secured its airtight yoke.

"Oh, yes." Khải laughed humorlessly. "A ritual." He pulled on his borrowed helm and continued the conversation through its comlink. "All cultures have their rituals, do they not, Lieutenant?"

"I guess," McKay muttered, wishing the man would drop it.

"And what we are about to do," Khải continued, caressing the assault rifle strapped across his chest, "is surely the oldest ritual of all."

#

New Saigon was a city in flames. It hardly seemed possible in an age of plastiform buildings, electric-powered transportation, fusion generators and beamed energy transmission; but Inferno was not Earth. Many buildings were constructed out of native wood, and many vehicles ran on methane or alcohol. Add to that mixture several dozen self-styled revolutionaries liberally tossing around firebombs the night before, stir vigorously, and *voila*, one family-sized bonfire.

People had stampeded through the packed-dirt streets of the low, sprawling town, screaming in uncontrolled panic, leaving their possessions behind, abandoning the city to its fate and heading down the river as the flames burned high into the early hours of the morning. But that had been last night. Now the fires burned in solitude, those not lucky enough to escape the flames left as smoldering corpses in the smoking wreckage.

The living remnant in the city was gathered into two armed camps. The Exiles under Châu Shou-Shin were holed up inside the Colonial Guard planetary armory, the largest building in New Saigon. Attack vehicles prowled the street without, waiting for the assault they expected from the constabulary unit out of Peiping, the nearest city, whom they assumed Khải's people had called. Khải's constables, meanwhile, were barricaded in the local Government Center, waiting for something more potent than a handful of riot police.

And on the river that bordered the city on the east, some of the more daring souls watched from the shelter of crudely-built wooden rafts to see if or when the two groups would finally decide to shoot it out. For hours, they had been disappointed: nothing had happened.

Until an ear-splitting sonic boom shattered every window left intact in the city.

The light-grey Fleet Marine lander bled off speed as it curved back around the rain-sodden fields west of the city, then came in low and slow two streets behind the armory, belching thick clouds of dark, electrostatically-charged smoke that obscured eye and electronic sensor alike. It hovered for a scant moment less than two meters above the street, vectored-thrust jets swirling the smoke around it as a rear egress hatch flew open and sixteen figures dropped into the darkness below. Its job done, the lander moved on to circle the armory, still trailing smoke, and headed west to the farmlands to touch down lightly on its VTOL jets.

Buried in gouts of impenetrable fog, the two attack vehicles on the street fired blindly and desperately, filling the air with missiles, explosive shells and laser pulses, until first one then the other exploded in an incandescent cloud of molten metal, as missiles tipped with chemical hyperexplosives found their weak spots. The two Marines responsible dropped their shoulder-fired launchers, unslung their autorifles, and ran to join the rest of the squad.

"Shamir," Gunny Wolczk radioed, "take your group and hit the rear entrance. The rest of you follow the LT and me."

Before he had finished speaking, a half-dozen PanAsians in CeeGee armor scrambled out of the front entrance firing rocket rifles at targets whose positions they only half-understood from their helmets' unfamiliar optics.

Dobbs and LeClerc swung around their gimbal-mounted, backpack-fed autoguns, received the signal tones from their helmet-gun targeting links, and opened up on the revolutionaries. Their nearly-recoilless, polymer autoguns spat out a deadly barrage of alternating tungsten penetrators and hyperexplosive twelve millimeter frag rounds, the one-two punch hammering through the thick armor and butchering the men within, turning the six defenders into scrap metal and scattered body parts in less than a second.

"Smoke, Peterson," Wolczk ordered. The PFC pulled a pair of canisters out of a belt pouch, jerked out their pins and tossed them through the big, open double doors, filling the entrance corridor with clouds of inky smoke that spread through the building as quickly as the fire had spread through the city.

With the entrance cleared, Dobbs ducked inside first, followed by Wolczk, while McKay and his two guests led the remainder of the group in, leaving LeClerc to guard the rear. Confused, unarmored Exiles, running helter-skelter through the hallways, balked at the sight of the invading Marines and tried to bring up appropriated weapons, or tried to turn and run the other way, but were either blown into hamburger by Dobb's gun or pumped with tantalum-core 6mm slugs from the others' rifles.

"Command station to the left," Hernandez announced, running up beside McKay, his armored boots ringing on the floor like hammerblows.

"Captain," McKay instructed, "go with Peterson and LeClerc and secure the command station. If you can, try to grab someone alive and find out if all of your people are being held in the detention cells downstairs. That's where we'll be headed. Call me if you find anything."

"As you say," the Guard officer agreed, noticeably more cooperative now that the adrenaline had begun to pump. "But I cannot promise I will be able to restrain myself with any of these vermin."

He headed off to the left, followed by the two Marines.

"He's a wonderful guy," Wolczk muttered to McKay over their private channel.

"Yeah. C'mon, Gunny, let's go find those thumb-fingered Ceegees." He switched over to Khải's channel. "You doing okay, Constable?"

"Fine, thank you," Khải said calmly, even as he spun on his heel and put a single round into an incoming rifleman.

McKay grinned. "I can see that you are. All right, Dobbs, take point. Casey, watch our backs."

The six men set off at a brisk trot, disdaining the nearby elevator banks for the emergency stairwell while PFC Casey covered their backs with another smoke grenade. The door to the stairwell was locked...and shortly it was nonexistent, after Dobbs let it have a top-to-bottom burst. He led the way and the others filed through behind him.

Glancing at Dobbs, McKay idly entertained the thought that the man must be wearing an industrial exoskeleton under his armor. Even with what had to be forty-five kilos of gun, armor and ammo, the big man took the stairs three at a time.

They reached the door to the detention level unopposed, Wolczk trying it and finding it locked. Dobbs was about to do his number on it when McKay got a transmission over his helmet comlink and put a restraining hand on the gunner's arm.

"Wait a second," McKay ordered. "What was that?"

"This is Captain Hernandez," the Argentinean repeated. "I have the command station secured, but your trooper Peterson is dead."

"Damn!" McKay hissed, feeling like he'd been kicked in the nuts. "Did... did you capture anyone alive?"

"Not yet. But the security scanners are working, I have the detention level on the screen. It appears that all of my men are being held there, and they are heavily guarded: a dozen men, five in armor, one with an assault cannon."

"What's the layout?"

"The ones in armor are patrolling the halls; the one with the heavy gun is on your right. The seven others are in the detention control center at the left end, about fifty meters down the hall."

"Can you gas the ones in the control center?" McKay asked hopefully.

"Negative. The gas cells are dry. If you will wait, we will come down to aid you..."

"No," McKay cut him off. "I need you to coordinate with Corporal Shamir. Get ahold of him, and let him know if there's any concentrations of enemy and where they are. Try to find Khải's people..."

"I can see them on the outside scanners already," Hernandez interrupted. "They're approaching the front entrance---about twenty of them."

"All right," McKay sighed. "Contact Corporal Shamir and get them working together. We're going to free your men. I'll call you when the smoke clears. McKay out."

He turned back to his half-squad. "All right, let's do it by the numbers. The second Dobbs takes out that door, I want Casey to toss in a smoke grenade. We got a gunner on the right, four others in armor up and down the hall, plus seven regulars at the end of the corridor. Nichols, you draw the gunner's fire, give Dobbs enough time to get in and nail him. Gunny, you and me'll try to take out the guys on the left quick with grenades. Watch your aim though, we got CeeGees on both sides of the hall.

"Casey, you and Khải wait until the hall is clear, then go take the detention control center. Use gas grenades if possible, but don't take any chances. Everybody ready?"

A chorus of "Aye sir," answered him as Casey pulled out his last smoke grenade. McKay fed a rocket-assisted antiarmor grenade into the launcher mated to the side of his autorifle, and the others followed his example. "Okay, Dobbs, do it!"

Dobbs squeezed the trigger of his weapon, lifting the muzzle from the base of the door upwards, blowing it into scattered bits of debris with a metallic roar. Casey chucked in his smoke bomb, then Nichols followed it through the doorway, rolling into a crouch in the center of a corridor lined with transparent plastiform cell doors. Clouds of smoke billowing around him, Nichols fired his grenade launcher by reflex at the first target he saw, an armored guard standing just to the right and in front of the assault gunner. The antiarmor grenade took the man at belt level and blew him in half in a deafening explosion that splattered everything within ten meters with blood and metal fragments.

The PanAsian gunner was momentarily startled, but he was also a combat veteran. He swung around his twenty-kilo weapon and fired two rounds at Nichols through the smoke. Even as the gunner was firing, Dobbs was squeezing through the stairwell door behind Nichols and more armored troops were running up from the left, taking wild shots at the incoming Marines.

The gunner's volley missed Nichols by a good meter, the rocket-assisted rounds impacting a cell door with a double-thunderclap, punctuated by the screams of the Guard soldiers within. Dobbs growled deep in his throat and hosed the gunner with a ten-round burst of twelve mil that chewed up the firing mechanism of the rebel's cannon before decapitating him.

Behind Dobbs, Wolczk and McKay intercepted the advancing armored troops with a pair of rocket grenades, each of them downing a man with explosions that shook the halls. That left one armored enemy, no time for the two Marines to reload their launchers, Constable Khải not yet through the doorway, and Dobbs facing the other direction.

"Dobbs!" was all McKay had time to say as he and Wolczk and the Asian revolutionary opened up with their rifles almost simultaneously.

McKay could see his shots ricocheting off the heavy armor on the man's chest and tried to adjust upward toward the faceplate, but a stream of smoke-trails was already erupting from the Exile's rocket rifle. All McKay could do was stare in helpless amazement as two of the fifteen mil, gyrostabilized minirockets punched through the honeycomb boron-ceramic armor over Wolczk's chest and blew a fist-sized hole in his back.

An eyeblink later, the gunner was dismembered by a long burst from Dobb's autogun, but Jason's horrified gaze was glued to the Gunny. His body seemed to float to the floor with impossible slowness, and through his faceplate Jason could see a look not of pain or fear but of profound confusion. Those squinting, half-alive eyes locked with McKay's, and for one, uncanny moment he felt frozen in time, as if Gunny Wolczk's death were such an unnatural thing that the universe wouldn't allow it to occur.   But then Wolczk's shoulders touched the floor, breaking the spell, and Casey and Khải took off at a double-time down the corridor toward the control center, leaving McKay and Dobbs gaping in disbelief at the lifeless body of Gunnery Sergeant Van Wolczk. McKay heard someone moaning softly, like a man slowly dying, and realized that it was coming from him.

Nichols, his brain whispered like some stranger clearing his throat for attention. *Where's Nichols?*

As if in response to his thoughts, an eddy of smoke rose from the floor to reveal PFC Arturo Nichols sprawled face-down a few meters away.

"Aw Jesus." McKay knelt beside him and gently turned the eighteen-year-old over, but he was gone, his throat blown out by a minirocket. "Dobbs!" McKay ordered through clenched teeth. "Go help Casey. Now!"

"Yes... aye, sir." The big man nodded slowly, tearing his gaze away from the Sergeant and turning to run down the corridor as gunshots sounded from the direction of the detention control center.

McKay left the two bodies and walked over to the cell door that had been shattered by the assault cannon. There were seven men inside of it, all dressed in the light-green duty fatigues of the Colonial Guard. Three of them were clearly dead, their uniforms shredded from the fragments both of the door and the Asian's cannon rounds. The other four were alive, but they had seen better days.

One was conscious: a slim, young east African with a broken and swollen nose and blood running from his left ear. He looked up at

McKay, blinking his eyes to clear them, and tried to get to his knees, coughing from the smoke drifting down the corridor.

"Who are you?" he asked in accented English.

"Marines," McKay told him over his helmet's external speaker. Offering a hand, he pulled the soldier to his feet. "Are you okay?"

He shook his head. "I can't hear you so good, but I want to fight them."

"Come on then," McKay urged, waving for the man to follow. The soldier grabbed a rocket rifle from one of the dead rebels and hefted the heavy weapon confidently.

McKay glanced around him. There were dozens of other Guard troops in the other cells in the corridor, pounding soundlessly, screaming without being heard behind the soundproof doors. Without a computer key card, McKay realized, there was no way to open the cells except from the control center. Jason signaled for them to wait with an upheld hand, and they seemed to relax.

"Casey, this is McKay," he radioed. "Sitrep."

"Control center is ours, sir," Casey reported. "We've got a couple live ones. They say Ngô Bảo Châu's somewhere on this level."

"Right. Stay there till you hear from Shamir. See if you can get the cell doors unlocked."

"We'll try, sir. It may take a while... some of the control boards were hit."

"Do your best."

"Sir," Casey wondered, "what about Châu?"

"Don't worry," McKay replied grimly. "I'm going to find him. McKay out." The Lieutenant turned to his new-found ally, who appeared to be getting impatient. "C'mon," he motioned. "We've got to find..." He was interrupted by the ringing echo of a gunshot, and a shrill scream somewhere off to his right. "Dammit!"

Jason took off headlong down the corridor with the African at his heels. Rounding a curve to the left, they saw a tall, rakishly-mustached Chinese male whom Jason recognized from the threat briefings as Ngô Bảo Châu calmly firing a pistol into an open cell of restrainer-bound Colonial Guard troops. Two were already dead, and he was lining up on a third...

"Son of a bitch!" Jason opened up with his autorifle, the deep-throated stutter of his weapon in sharp contrast with the muted cough of the young Guardsman's rocket rifle.

The Exile leader danced backwards under the impact of half a magazine of McKay's six mil slugs before a pair of minirockets blew his skull apart like a water balloon. The African soldier, his eyes wide and wild, kept pumping round after round into the corpse until his weapon went dry. What was left of Châu by the time the rifle's ammo drum hit empty bore little resemblance to a human being.

By instinct more than anything else, McKay swept the area with his helmet sensors, but saw only more imprisoned Guard troops. Letting out a deep sigh, Jason felt a shudder run through him, all the fear and anger and hatred welling up inside his gut, rising like gorge in his throat.

It shouldn't have happened like this. They had done everything by the book, no mistakes, but Gunny and the rest were still dead. McKay had to shake his head to dispel the memory of the experienced Gunnery Sergeant greeting his new Lieutenant, merged with the lingering image of the same man's limp and lifeless body. Eventually, he realized that someone was speaking to him over his helmet comlink.

"...tenant McKay, are you there, sir?" It was Shamir.

"I'm here. Report." He was surprised at how calm his voice was.

"The base is clean, sir." Shamir's voice told of physical and emotional exhaustion. "No resistance left anywhere if Captain Hernandez is reading the sensors correctly." A long pause, and McKay could hear him taking a deep breath. "We lost Corson and Dundee. Richards and Mitchell are wounded, but they should both pull through."

"Call the lander," McKay ordered, fighting to keep his brain working just a little longer. "Have them contact the *Bradley,* send out a medical unit. Get Khải's people to set up a temporary hospital till we can evac the wounded. Get some stretchers down to the detention level, some of the CeeGees'll need treatment."

"Aye, sir."

"Oh, and Shamir..." McKay trailed off, his voice catching in his throat. "You're acting Sergeant."

"Uh...yes, sir. I'm sorry, sir."

Jason leaned heavily against the wall and slid slowly down to the floor. He knew he should help the young African untie the CeeGees. He knew he should gather up his men and get them to the command center... but not just now.

#

It was about a half an hour later before McKay, Casey and Dobbs made their way back up to the command center, leaving Khải and his cops on the detention level to care for the wounded. Small fires burned in places and the corridors were filled with drifting smoke that coated the walls with soot. Bodies of rebels, and a few of local police, littered the hallways, but McKay studiously avoided looking at them.

As the three Marines approached the entrance to the command center, they heard the sounds of some kind of disturbance from their destination: shouts, crashing furniture, and the unmistakable sound of flesh striking flesh. McKay was too drained to hurry, he just continued walking at a normal gait toward the wide, open doorway.

"Tell me!" Hernandez's voice reached them before they came to the entrance. "Tell me where he is!" The smack of a fist into flesh echoed off the walls.

McKay came to the doorway and saw the brawny Guard Captain, sans armor, clutching a bound Vietnamese teenager by the shirtfront with one hand and slapping him with the other. Blood was already flowing from the youth's nose and mouth, and he looked only half-conscious.

"Captain Hernandez." McKay pulled off his helmet and tossed it and his rifle to Casey. "Just what are you doing with that Marine prisoner?" His voice was soft, but deadly as a loaded gun.

"McKay, you..." Hernandez spun around, but hesitated in mid-bluster. The grim set of McKay's jaw was enough to give even the arrogant Guard Captain pause. "I was attempting to force the whereabouts of Ngô Bảo Châu from this Exile scum we captured."

"Put him down," McKay ordered.

"I will have the truth from him," Hernandez insisted, voice rising like a child denied a toy. "That Goddamned gook is responsible for my personal humiliation! Having to run from the city like a child..."

"I said," McKay repeated, stepping up and punching the Captain full in the face with a straight left, "put him down!"

Hernandez pitched over backward, hands going to his nose, while his prisoner slumped to his knees. The Guard Captain spat out a red blob, swearing through clenched teeth as he struggled to his feet.

"Bastard!" Hernandez started into a lunge for McKay, but Corporal Shamir appeared like a wraith, interposing his autorifle between the two officers.

"Don't," was all the Israeli said.

"Ngô Bảo Châu is dead," McKay told Hernandez, his voice more tired than angry. "I killed him, with the help of one of your men. Remember your men, Captain? The reason we didn't just bomb this building to rubble? The reason I just got five good people killed? I'll tell you one thing, Hernandez, it sure as hell wasn't to save your reputation. Why don't you go and see to your men, Captain? Why don't you just get the hell out of my sight?"

Hernandez looked as if he were about to say something, but reconsidered after a glance at Shamir's assault rifle. Wiping a hand across his chin, the Captain turned on his heel and stomped out of the room.

McKay stepped over to the other side of the command center, where the two wounded Marines rested. Richards, a hard-muscled woman with hair shorter than McKay's and skin the color of dark chocolate, leaned against the wall with half-closed eyes, her left thigh swathed in a thick field bandage. Mitchell, a wiry, pale teenager who'd joined their squad at the same time as McKay, was stretched out unconscious, an oxygen mask over his face and a soaked-through dressing taped to his right side. Jean LeClerc, bereft of both his helmet and his autogun, was leaning over Mitchell, checking his vital signs with a small, electronic sensor.

"How is he?" McKay asked the French-Canadian.

LeClerc shrugged. "Lost a lot of blood. Got maybe three shattered ribs, a punctured right lung. He'll live, but he could use some attention, and soon." McKay nodded then went over to squat beside Richards.

"How're you doing, Private Richards?"

"Feeling no pain, sir," she said, grinning, eyes slightly out of focus. "Jean's got me pumped with some good shit."

"Her femur's broken," Jean told him, "but the artery's still intact. She'll be fine. They'll have it fused and she'll be walking in a few days."

"Good." Jason patted her on the shoulder. "You take it easy. The medtechs'll be here soon."

McKay straightened and moved to where Shamir was leaning on the commo board, talking to the lander. Jason sat on the edge of the panel and waited for the Corporal to finish. The young Israeli finally signed off and looked over to his Lieutenant.

"Lander says the medevac team'll be here in five minutes, sir."

"You did a good job taking this place," McKay told him honestly.

Shamir just nodded. His short, black hair was matted with sweat, and there were lines of exhaustion in his face. "Sir..." He trailed off helplessly.

"What?" McKay prompted.

"I don't understand why they did it, sir," he said, shaking his head. "They had to know they couldn't hold this place. Why didn't they just hit it and fade back into the crowd? Why wait here and get slaughtered?"

Jason started to answer, but hesitated. In a moment like this, did the young corporal really want to hear his college professor's theories of terrorist tactics and symbolic martyrdom? Hell, what did that professor know about death?

"It's just a ritual, Ari," he sighed. "Just a ritual."

-o-

Rick Partlow is a former US Army Infantry officer who attended Florida Southern College and has written eight novels and several short stories. He currently lives in central Florida.

Homepage: **https://rickpartlow.wordpress.com**

First Generation

by Adrien Walker

Gabriel Benson stood before the man, though man wasn't entirely accurate. No new title existed, nothing with which to call himself, Gabriel knew it to be intentional. The man, or rather, the rebel, was no longer a man. He transformed, changing himself down to the bone. He became thin, almost to the point of appearing impossibly so. The skin decayed, peeled back over muscle, both now green. The bones, visible across much of his appearance, especially in his limbs, and those that constructed his rib cage, became black. His eyes evolved into two black balls resting in a head so deteriorated it was essentially a green skull. And so he was named, for his very appearance. Green Skull. The rebel leader, the forefather of the coming race. But it had yet to arrive, and therefore remained nameless.

Green Skull slowly dressed himself, pulling his black military garments over his body, slipping each limb carefully into the cloth, then zipping up along the center to unite two sides of a large symbol: a hand, green like his flesh, painted across his chest.

Gabriel observed his leader with reverence, ensuring he withheld any affect of disgust. In truth, he hadn't much to repress, having been predisposed to much of Green Skull's body already. As the rebel leader's closest commander, Gabriel observed the intimate thoughts of Green Skull in rare moments. Green Skull offered little, but what comfort Green Skull could show in the company of others, Gabriel stood as sole confidant.

"Don't fret, it's not your future," Green Skull hissed, his voice pouring through the holes in his neck as much as it emitted from his mouth. With absent lips, the flesh shriveled back over his teeth, though with remarkably coherent speech, trained so with diligence. Discipline attracted Gabriel to the man in the first place. A quality lacking in Diamond City's Scouts. His disenchantment with humanity's final bastion began months prior, when corruption led to his abdication. In circles of other dissenters, he first heard of the half-zombie. Of course, they abandoned the term, since pledging their allegiance to the Green Hand rebellion. As Gabriel stared into the black eyes of his leader he thought back to their meeting and the months leading to this moment. A lifetime, a friendship, an education. Everything wrapped into it, and now he gave his body over to it all. He would be the first.

"I'm not afraid," Gabriel replied, his broad chest raised. His body appeared nearly a perfect opposite to Green Skull. Gabriel's massive frame stretched six and a half feet tall. Vibrant flesh wrapped it, a red which deepened with any expression. Large muscles adorned his structure, and his posture accentuated his strength. Yet he banished arrogance as he stood in the center of the room, a dimly lit section of tunnel far beneath the city. Its grim quality shown across its walls, covered in decades old filth, and in the flickering light dangling from a rope above, running off siphoned power from the city of their betrayal. Yet, in Gabriel's eyes, he enshrined the setting with glory.

Other men stood huddled around, the inner circle chosen in accordance with Gabriel and Green Skull's private discussions on loyalty and value. They watched the ceremony, both with eagerness and a sense of curiosity for the thing they all promised to partake in. In some of their hearts, no doubt, some fear lingered. Gabriel knew, he'd experienced it himself. He assuaged it the closer to Green Skull he grew.

An elderly man, the only other standout beside Green Skull, cautiously handled a concoction on a table off center in the room. His back curved into a hunch, impeding his arm's fluidity, though his fingers acted with a finesse unmatched. His eyes followed them, transferring the fluids from a variety of sources into a funnel which wound them through tubing into a final destination, a small bowl beneath the chemistry set-up. He watched the liquids religiously as they combined, a black, thick liquid, funneling into a thinner red, a pristine white, and finally a cloudy green which dominated the ultimate mixture with its glowing hue. The room's collective gaze fell upon him in the silence after Green Skull redressed, though he continued unfazed, ensuring his measurements for the final cocktail. Once it completed, he gave a solitary nod towards Green Skull, who then raised his hand and lowered it, signalling to Gabriel.

A deep breath entered Gabriel's nose, a now sweaty appendage that he could feel radiating with heat as he turned bright red. His heart slammed against his rib cage with each beat. It wasn't fear. He had erased it. It was exhilaration.

He turned and raised his leg onto the edge of a small, rectangular table behind him. Its metal surface chilled his back as he laid onto it, though the sweat continued to roll along his flesh, cooling once it met with the table. Green Skull fastened a series of restraints, dismissing the others from doing so. He methodically wrapped the leather bindings around Gabriel's wrists and ankles, tightening, then checked with Gabriel to guarantee they were fastened well. For each, Gabriel offered a tug, then nodded to the adequacy of his restraints. When he finished, Green Skull laid his boney hand across Gabriel's bare chest, planting it there. Gabriel felt the rough edges where the bones of each knuckle wore against one another, the smooth texture of the muscles that bound them, the rough flesh that scarcely remained, stretched over bits of palm. The hand tapped against him, as Green Skull lowered his mouth to Gabriel's ear. "This was all just a vessel," he whispered.

Gabriel released his breath. "On its way to the ultimate."

Green Skull nodded and the smallest curl appeared at the corner of Gabriel's mouth. Then Green Skull looked up to the elderly man and called him forth by his name. "Dr. Gregory McIntyre." He stepped back, inviting the doctor to the side of the restrained Gabriel Benson. "Please escort Commander Benson into the First Generation."

The doctor rounded the edge of the metal table atop which Gabriel lay naked and restrained. In his right hand, Gregory's long, thin fingers wrapped around a syringe and its barrel, filled with the concoction. As he lowered the pointed end towards Gabriel's bulging vein running through the inside of his elbow, pulsating with increased bloodflow, lifting and lowering the flesh running over it, Gabriel had the instinct to twist the frail doctor's arm and snap it from his body.

A strange thought, he considered, unable to trace its origin, but its presence influenced the muscles of his arm, which flexed against the restraints. He gritted his teeth, blowing air through his nostrils, hot as it washed over his upper lip, trying in essence to expel the blasphemous thought. His eyes rolled over to the men in attendance, their curious gazes falling on his every motion. Several suddenly wore concern, watching the lurching motion of their commander. Their feet tapped nervously, some turned unconsciously, several more grimaced.

Gabriel took a deep breath, in through his nose, the sweat dripping from its end, falling within. Then he exhaled, pushing out a long breath through his pursed lips.

He turned his arm, commanding it with strained effort, both against the restraints and his instincts, to better position it for the needle. He sought to erase the previous weakness, to show the men he was ready, that it was mere eagerness. He was not frightened. Fear no longer existed within his heart, which pounded louder against his chest, and now in his ears. No. More. Fear.

His nose pushed the air out from his chest in short bursts, the sweat ran along the bridge like a river in the valley above his upper lip. He ground his upper and lower jaws. Gregory stared into his eyes with hesitation.

Shaking, Gabriel pushed the inside of his elbow up nearer to the needle's point.

"Doctor," he spoke, quietly urging.

Gregory looked over to Green Skull, who returned his stare without a change in presentation. He stood with arms crossed, chin raise, posture perfect, and eyes black watching unwaveringly. Gabriel twisted his head to view his leader, an upside down portrait of the rebel he had followed into this moment, whose speeches on the evolution of humanity into its next phase and the sacrifices required for its transition lit a fire in his mind. His skull felt aflame now, his flesh checkered with beads of perspiration, his scalp itchy.

He felt a pinch and then a rush. He tore his eyes away from Green Skull towards his arm, watching while the concoction was thrust into his vein by the depressing thumb of Dr. Gregory McIntyre, hunched closer, watching intently.

Then the heat, the fire, the sweat, the heartbeat, went cold, like the sweat beads against the table. The room disappeared behind a cloud of black, and he saw, for a moment, a visage of himself, naked, small, being swallowed in the dark. He thought he could hear his own voice calling to him, cursing, but it was gone as soon as it appeared. When he was gone from sight, the world returned, still.

He looked around at the wide eyes as he took his first breath as a member of the first generation. Though, as the air rushed through his nose, he felt the flesh, the cartilage deteriorate, rapidly caving, then molting, like snakeskin, drifting off his face with his exhale. His eyes felt pressured, his vision was wider, deeper. He lifted his head from the back of the table to peer down along his body. His flesh was grey, its previous reddened color rushing away towards his feet as the new tone conquered him.

Gregory cautiously unlatched Gabriel's right arm, then shuffled back, watching Gabriel's eyes. Then, after a moment, Gregory rushed towards the other side. Gabriel paused him, raising his right hand. The doctor stopped, staring back at Green Skull, who remained statuesque. Gabriel looked down at the restraint, then flexed his arm. He pulled against it, snarling with effort, but in a pair of seconds he was freed of his own volition. The action repeated twice more for his ankles, which he threw over the edge to hop off the table.

He was different, he knew this, he could feel it. He could feel a surge of power filling his body, his muscles made more efficient, just as he had been told they would be. His vision contained the ability to analyze his environment, counting its elements, and categorizing the terrain, just as he had expected. His hearing, too, improved, listening to the hum of the electricity as it powered the lights, following its buzz through the roof above him.

He changed, and yet, as he stared into the aghast expressions of the men in the room, desperate to hide their emotions but failing to do so, he didn't feel so detached. He felt as though a mirror would reveal the same shock in his face, in spite of its new appearance. He knew their thoughts and heard the same in his own mind.

His eyes found a young man at the front, his tiny frame shivering at the sight of the creature before him. Gabriel stepped closer towards him, finding him more a boy than a man. He gravitated towards him for reasons unknown, though in his posture attempted to convey an intention of assuaging fear. Then he laid his hand upon the shoulder of the boy. Through the uniform, he could feel the heat, his palm experienced the intensity of the boy's heart. And in feeling the fear in the boy, he could feel none of the sensations in himself. His heartbeat was missing, there was only cold in his flesh. All the impassioned sensations in the moments before the needle plunged into his vein, all the distinctly human feelings that flooded his body with warmth and tingling, vanished. And Commander Benson knew they were never to return.

He suddenly felt miles from the boy, despite their contact. He lowered his hand, dropped his arm to his side, then lifted his chin.

"We are the harbingers of the future race, son," he told the boy, words spoken now from the truth that replaced his heartbeat. He spoke rhetoric, almost meaningless, and yet the only meaning in the world. It fuelled him before, fed his loyalty through his heart, through his love. These things became trite now. *His body was just a vessel.* Its creations of humanity were false idols, used for their own demise.

He wanted to laugh, how much sense it made now, in the absence of all what drove him to it. But humor, too, seemed moot.

He really only felt work now, and the desire to complete it.

He felt Green Skull behind him, lifting the sleeves of his commander's uniform to feed his arms through. He allowed Green Skull to lift it over his body, zipping the center up from his belly to his neck, adorning his chest with the Green Hand emblem.

"Your commanding officer, gentlemen. Commander Benson."

Slowly, the men in attendance began to clap, first a hollow gesture, then building, accompanied with hollers and whistles, their human naivete on exhibition. Commander Benson and Green Skull exchanged knowing glances. Then the leader stepped forth, joining his newly inducted commander at his side.

"Now, are there any in attendance who do not wish to proceed? Here today are those most loyal to the Green Hand, our personally chosen, selected for their loyalty, their value, and their determination for the cause. If even one of you is to shy from this, it would destroy the ranks before we ever had a chance. So, understand this. I will dismiss you, but you must approach now."

Commander Benson watched the crowd grow silent as Green Skull paced behind him, hands cradling one another behind his back. The men strained to reflect their devotion, though there was not one among them who hadn't perspired to a degree that it dripped along their bright flesh, a telltale sign of their inner world, racing with emotion, with fear intermingling. Moments, only, and yet a vast gulf separated Commander Benson from the lot.

A trembling man stepped forth, his chin shivering, chattering his teeth in a grating rhythm to Commander Benson's new hearing.

"Harold Usadel." Green Skull approached the man, observing him from an inch's distance. "You wish not to proceed."

The rebel scout nodded his head, then burst into tears. The men behind him grinned, several laughing. Green Skull stepped forth, past Harold and in towards their faces.

"Not one of you hasn't what Harold shows us now. It is the pity of the human race, and an unfortunate burden for those beneath its banner." Green Skull rested his stripped hand onto Harold's shoulder as it quivered with the boy's sobbing. In a whispered tone, and hung head, Green Skull spoke more gently into Harold's ear, "What I wouldn't give to feel as you do again, and feel it for the rest of my days." He sighed. "But I have given and will continue to give so much more for something immensely greater." Green Skull caught Commander Benson's eye once more, a glance and a brief communication. Green Skull lifted his hand from Harold's shoulder and addressed the crowd, "Evolution is sacrifice."

Commander Benson clapped his fists into the sides of Harold's skull, cracking it and causing blood to rush from his eye sockets as their stare went blank. His body dropped to the floor. Commander Benson looked into it crumpled at his feet. He felt nothing. His only thought came as the consideration of his own like fate at some future time.

Then he observed a subsequent thought. Between then and now, there was much work to be done.

-o-

Adrien Walker is the writer of post-apocalyptic, thriller, horror, and scifi books that seek to capture dark thematic elements and explore them to their wildest conclusions. From zombies lumbering about a barren landscape, to a space station floating in the vastness of space, he explores the nature of species, of humanity, and what it means to be alive. He loves works that do the same, introducing questions that have audiences scratching their skulls for days.

Homepage: **https://adrienwalker.com**

Mailing List: **https://adrienwalker.com/books/zevolution-series/first-generation**

The Grape Thieves

by Corrie Garrett

Irina rested her foot on a low bench and sneezed. The plants in the labyrinth tickled her allergies, or perhaps it was the fresh air itself. The very freshest air on the whole ship surrounded her, shoved through one point two miles of tightly coiled corridors lined with fern, ivy, azalea, and other top-of-the-line air purifiers.

She'd passed a group of adolescents cleaning sun bulbs, and a group of even tinier kids harvesting grape tomatoes. The labyrinth was crawling with children every day, one of the few ways to build tolerances on the *Aegea*. Irina herself had grown up on another Diadem ship, perhaps that was why her eyes streamed when she approached this place and she even felt vaguely claustrophobic here in a way no other part of the ship affected her.

She would never admit that to anyone; she was no victim to be tormented by claus, the worst of the mental illnesses in her opinion.

She could touch both walls at once with her hands, and the ceiling was only a foot above her head, but that was not unusual, and she refused to allow the dangling greenness of it all to perturb her.

Irina was tall and sturdy, not an ideal body type on any of the Diadem ships, but her mind was as sturdy as her body and she would never allow irrational fears to rule her.

In this section of the labyrinth, gourds dangled like undersize punching bags from scaffolds on the ceiling. Racks on the walls held herbs interspersed with lilies, and here, at least, it all looked healthy. She sneezed again and continued further in.

Although it was called the labyrinth, there was no way to get lost in here. One tunnel, all the way through. Positive pressure from the center kept the air flowing outward to the rim. If you did get confused or disoriented, you only needed to lick your finger and hold it up. The windward side was further in, leeward side was the way out. That was what they told the children anyway.

Irina took a sharp left, and then another one as she followed the path. Although it was barely more than a mile long, it felt like much more with all the twists and turns.

The Aegeans swore the purification of the labyrinth made their ship the healthiest of all.

Irina had her doubts as to the true benefit of this monstrosity. After all, her own home ship, the *Griffin*, had not had a labyrinth and their children were not stunted from formaldehyde build-up or lack of systemic challenge to the immune system. She was taller than most of the men on the *Aegea*, for heaven's sake.

At the next turn, the herbs gave way to rows and rows of green onions. It was a Smell. A handful of kids wielded scissors, trimming them down to the dirt and stacking the green shoots on a large plastic tray. One child simply sat, with her hands limply in her lap, and a distant look on her face. One finger twitched rhythmically.

Irina had to turn sideways to edge by them, and the kids paused to look up at her with their mouths open; except for the one little girl. Perhaps she was one of the kids off the *Rumi*. Irina had heard there were behavioural problems already. But what could you expect after what they'd been through?

As the path turned again, she heard one of the kids whisper, "Hoo, she's big."

Irina's mouth quirked up. She was fairly certain her size had carried her application to the top of the pile for peacekeeping officers.

During the Pauses, when the eight ships of the Diadem stopped accelerating for a few months, a great shuffling occurred. The individual ships, which usually travelled far apart to minimize risk, all linked up to the *Necklace*, creating a brief window of opportunity.

Pauses happened every twenty years, allowing for the mingling and rearranging of the population and resources of the ships. They were a Herculean feat of organization. The ship captains and a host of section heads synchronized transition, repair, redistribution, transfer requests, competitive games… anything and everything that could help the ships and the passengers handle another twenty years of space travel.

Irina had been ready. Her application was filed months before the Pause began. She was told not to get her hopes up. The *Aegea* was shaping up to be particularly popular; there were unaccountable swings in desirability during each Pause.

But Irina had included her physical stats (optional) and had gotten an interview only two weeks into the Pause. That was even after the shock of finding out that the *Rumi* had suffered catastrophic losses and the remaining passengers would have to be divvied up among the other ships.

Now here she was. Of course, she was the lowest ranking officer on the peacekeeping force, besides being an outsider, but she'd expected to pay her dues. She was on a trial run until the end of the Pause and she was determined not to get kicked back to the *Griffin* for the next twenty years.

As low man on the team, hiking to the center of the labyrinth and staking it out tonight had fallen to her. There were reports that someone was stealing from the depths of the labyrinth. She didn't yet know exactly how the record keeping worked with this place, it seemed a mess to her, but several supervisors had confirmed the theft over the last two weeks.

They'd stationed guards at the mouth of the labyrinth, but no one was coming out with extra. The kids who came and went were searched, and they all swore up and down they hadn't eaten a thing. Visitors from the other ships were only allowed in the labyrinth with an escort. The guards had begun giving breathalyzer tests, and they said no one was coming out with malic or citric acid on their breath either.

Irina had her doubts about all the kids in here, but at least a stakeout could tamp down some of the speculation.

Irina carried a sack on one shoulder with her water bottle, hard rations, and a tablet. The chief told her she might as well finish reading the Aegean Code of Misdemeanors and Petty Crimes. She'd already worked her way through Felonies, Endangerment, and

Deterrence: Aegean Judicial Rulings. And of course she'd studied the basic guidelines for peacekeepers, scanned a welcome booklet for new citizens of the *Aegea*, and a glanced at a book called Life Transitions and Emotional Health on the Diadem, which was required reading for all who switched ships.

Until today, Irina had only been in the mouth of the labyrinth, and that only a few times. It was a popular place for Aegeans to show off to strangers, just as the people on her ship showed off the cricket field.

The cricket field, an unbroken expanse of grass carefully cultivated from a clump of weeds found in a dung container, was one of the *Griffin's* only claims to fame. Anything that took up an egregious amount of space and resources tended to become one of the wonders of the Diadem. And strangers from the other ships usually exclaimed with polite amazement, while they inwardly scoffed at the waste of space. Each visitor wondered why they'd used their limited space for *this*. Instead of something sensible.

Irina arrived at the other end of the labyrinth about thirty-five minutes later. The tunnel opened out into a round room, perfectly elliptical like an egg. The sloping walls and roof and even the floor gave her a vertig assault, but at least it was a little wider here. Red, plastic cones blocked off the entrance to the egg room, and Irina stepped around them. The floor was covered with creeping herbs, except for a few paving 'stones,' synthetically produced by the ship's 3D printers.

The stones looked and felt 'down,' but as she stepped in, her perspective shifted and instead the tunnel became slightly down, like a rabbit hole slanting into a hill. This end of the labyrinth was near the core of the ship, and the rotational gravity became a bit wonky here. Or rather: it decreased in the exact ratio as defined by the circumference and velocity of the ship's spin, but the human inner ear didn't understand that ratio. So the mind often forced perspective shifts like a good Escher painting.

It was worse on the *Aegea* than the *Griffin*. Of the eight Diadem ships, the biggest was the *Necklace*, of course. Then there were four disc ships, including the *Griffin*, and then three smaller spike ships. The *Aegea* was one of the small ones.

Irina rubbed her eyes and turned slowly in place to let her body adjust. There were no children in this part of the labyrinth, and the loudest sound was the drip of the water in the molecule lines. A soft shushing came from the vents that lined the upper portion of the egg. This was where the air was forced into the labyrinth. There was no exit or entrance for people on this end. Only one entrance, one point two miles behind her. Deep breath.

If she didn't allow claus thoughts to form, she wouldn't succumb. Being big, Irina had faced more than the average number of taunts and challenges. She'd once spent fifteen hours in a clothes recycler on a dare. She'd fallen asleep, actually, otherwise she never would have made it so long. She still held the *Griffin* record.

Irina sat on one of the paving stones and leaned back against the curving walls, resting her head against a vent. It blew her short hair around her ears and cooled her neck and back.

She could see where the thieves had been. The vents were crisscrossed by gnarled grapevines trained onto plastic frames. Many glossy green leaves had been torn off and littered the floor. They stood out among the darker greens and textures of the herbs. Even some of the grape vines themselves had been half-pulled from the walls. One vine as thick as her wrist dangled from a scrap of bark. Only a few sad grape clusters could be seen, and Irina had been assured that there should still be many.

The egg room was special, often a place where marriage proposals were made, and newborns consecrated. With dispensation from the gardeners, the event could even take place here, and the bride and groom ate a single grape to celebrate and commemorate the moment.

Well, there weren't many left and that made the Aegeans angry.

The Pause would end soon. There were a lot of intent-to-marry contracts being signed and a lot of people wanted to use the egg. And of course in another nine to twelve months, those who had gotten married would start presenting their little bundles here.

Irina had to admit, if this was the work of kids, they'd been greedy little beasts about it, and quite stupid, too.

Who would notice a stolen grape here or there? If they wanted to snatch a few, they could do it without causing so much trouble.

Now it had become a sensation. An omen, even. This was the second to last Pause in their journey. In forty years, God willing, the Diadem would arrive at Sirius II. Irina would be sixty-five. The Diadem life expectancy was eighty-one, so she had a good shot at making it. That thought was growing on everyone under the age of fifty: I could MAKE it.

The idea of a mutated crop disease was an unspoken but lasting terror, so the more violent aspects of this grape problem had been widely publicized, lest anyone fear a microbial pest.

That decision made sense, as far as it went, but now people were talking about the "beast" of the labyrinth.

Something aggravated and selfish like this was viewed with deep misgiving. And Lord help the stupid soul responsible, because the Aegeans would not be forgiving of the person who sullied the excitement of the Pause.

Irina stretched. Her back was already stiff from the unnatural curve.

Truly, this was the most uncomfortable place. No wonder Mauricio had laughed and grimaced when she told him her assignment was to stay the night. He was at least eighteen inches shorter than her, it would probably be easy for him to curl up and rest in here.

Not that she was going to rest. Irina intended to keep her eyes wide open. If any thief did show up, she'd catch him. She would not foul up her shot on the Aegea.

#

After several hours, the smell of onions and herbs had abated considerably. Irina's nose must have adjusted. She unwrapped a hardbar and nibbled on it while she tapped through the long document.

The rations tasted different here. The bar was salty, rather than sweet, with chunks of olives and dates mixed into the protein. It was a weird flavor, but then she hadn't changed ships to maintain normalcy.

The sun lamps had gone dark three hours ago, and only tiny LEDs in the floor offered any light beyond her tablet. And those were mostly obscured by foliage.

Irina lay back on the floor as she chewed and propped her feet against a section of vent. That was a bit better for her stiff spine but still not ideal. Plus, her head dangled off the flat, plastic stone uncomfortably. She scooted down, but now the edge of the rock cut into her lower back.

Irina wedged her water bottle under her butt and sighed.

It was going to be a long night. Supposedly no one knew she was here except a few of the peacekeepers. Even the kids she'd passed were to be told she'd left early if they asked. Mauricio was the guy stationed at the entrance tonight and he would probably work it in even if they didn't ask.

A slight clicking noise filled the egg.

Irina froze. From her vantage point on the floor, she could see the whole curved vent. While sitting here in the semi-dark, alone, she had indulged a few creepy speculations about those vents. They were the obvious other entrance, if anything *was* entering, and thoughts of mutated rats or other horrors had given her a few shivers. There were no rats on the *Aegea* or the *Griffin*, but she'd heard rumors of an infestation on the *Necklace* and they *were* linked up now...

But the clicking sound, though it came and went, did not grow louder. The vents didn't so much as shudder.

Nothing was coming through.

Irina slowly sat up. She'd allowed her tablet light to go off, so it was quite dark now.

She clicked on her wrist light: a tiny white LED on a strap that every crewman and passenger wore. A quick sweep around the vents confirmed it; absolutely nothing.

She was facing away from the tunnel when she felt the hair on her neck stand up. Maybe it was the slightest breath of air going the wrong way, or maybe it was a primal human response to unseen eyes, but she knew something had come.

Irina swung toward the tunnel, her light and taser in front.

Flickering movement, but near the ceiling. Her eyes focused upward, and she yelped.

Long, jointed, hairy legs. Sparkly, multifaceted eyes. Shiny carapace peeking out from stiff bristles.

Spiders? Beetles?

There was a trail of them, and the foremost was almost directly overhead. Irina could not retreat further. She bent her knees and shifted a little to the right. The insect-thing didn't react, but kept crawling. One hairy leg after the other. It was huge and unspeakably awful. It had to be as big as her two hands together, and she didn't have tiny hands.

The vine it clung to ripped partly away from the ceiling and the monster swung inches from her face.

Irina felt like she might choke on her tongue. Or puke. Her heart might pound its way into her stomach.

But she didn't move. The spider found its footing and crawled back up the branch to the ceiling.

Another was just behind it.

A third was exiting the tunnel.

Irina squatted down and swallowed the growing amount of fear-induced spit in her mouth.

She counted five spiders altogether. They began cutting and (ugh!) sucking the last few of the grapes.

It was her duty to watch and document this problem, nightmare, more like, but she was on the brink of leaving a dozen times.

Claustrophobia was the worst of the mental sicknesses, sure, but Irina didn't have that. For the first time, she understood the nerve-level horror that people described. She had never felt this kind of utter revulsion. It was so strong it tasted of metal and set her thighs to shaking. Was this how Ellen had felt in a closet? Irina hoped not.

There were other animals on the Diadem, she had never reacted like this. There were even bee pollinators on three of the ships, so she was familiar with insects.

But these…

Irina shuddered and swallowed. She ought to get a picture maybe, but it was hard to move.

The thought of one of those hairy legs touching her shoulder, her hair, or, bah, her face nearly undid her.

Somehow, she managed to wait while they finished their nightly meal.

They started back toward the tunnel by some unspoken agreement.

The last, and biggest one, crawled back across the floor, inches from her kneeling legs. It looked even more ungainly upright than it had while hanging.

And how did these things get here? She'd heard nothing about spiders on the *Aegea*, and she would have, if this were known. Like the big bats on the *Griffin* or the tiny goats on the *Drake*.

Irina followed their progression, first just with her eyes, and then on foot. Where would they go?

She left several feet between her and the last one. She tried not to consider how fast it could move and how quickly it could swarm back down the tunnel and up into her face…

Every time they turned a corner, she half expected they would have disappeared, but they were always still in sight. Shiny, hard shells reflected her light.

They seemed to have no interest in losing her.

She'd lost track of how far they'd gone when she turned onto a longer corridor and smacked her head against something hard.

It swung out of the way, but still hurt. Irina put up a hand felt the smooth, cool rind of a squash.

Of course, she'd noticed these before.

The hanging vegetables cast weird shadows, but at least this part of the labyrinth was fairly straight. She stopped to give the spiders more space.

They weaved down the row, now on the wall, now on the ceiling. Irina would see this in nightmares for the rest of her life, she was certain. The third spider mistakenly got on one of the gourds and swung like a drunkard, twitching a horrible leg in the air.

And then... it slipped inside a seam in the gourd. First a leg or two, then its body, and finally it drew the last few legs in, a birth in reverse.

In her dim light, it disappeared. How did it fit? *Why* did it fit?

She watched carefully as the others followed suit, each with their own hanging nest. They must fold themselves up impressively to fit inside.

Did they hollow out those gourds for this purpose? And no one noticed?

When the spiders where entirely hidden from sight, Irina forced herself to take a closer look. There was a seam alright, but nothing was visible but puckered rind.

Earlier she'd ducked around these carelessly, even playfully swung one with her hand.

How did the crazy Aegeans not know about this? An infestation was a Big Deal. Any unregulated explosion of animal life was going to use resources allotted for other purposes. Possibly catastrophically. She'd only seen five spiders, but there were undoubtedly more. In the labyrinth? In the air ducts or the recycling chutes?

But... if the spiders were an endemic problem, there should have been signs of their feeding before the last few weeks. Had they only recently been introduced?

Anyone who saw one of those crawling along a hall or out of a vent would have notified someone. After they stopped screaming.

And why did they eat grapes? Surely that wasn't the crop they'd grown to adulthood on.

With a roll of nausea, it hit her that perhaps these weren't adults, as she assumed, but infants.

It was too much. Irina stumbled backward and then turned to retrace her steps to the egg and retrieve her things. Her stakeout was done. She knew the answer.

#

When she got back to Nightmare Row, as Irina now mentally dubbed the spider's lair, she was not ashamed of crouching and scurrying to the other end.

By the time she got to the labyrinth exit, Irina was walking confidently again. Her gait lengthened, her neck straightened, and her arms swung, perhaps a touch mechanically, but they swung, darn it.

Mauricio sat comfortably, cross-legged, in the medium-sized hall outside. The blessedly clean, straight lines of the hall seemed brightly lit compared to the labyrinth. All the nighttime LEDs weren't shrouded in leaves out here.

Mauricio looked up from his tablet in surprise, with his ready smile. "What? Solved already?"

His eyes were perhaps a bit deeper-looking than normal, more shadows, but otherwise he showed no sign of staying up half the night on a hard floor.

Perhaps her confidence was more ragged than she realized, because he immediately got to his feet and the smile disappeared. When he stood, his head barely reached her neck.

"Are you alright? Something happened?" He gripped her elbow, perhaps to comfort her, and Irina automatically shook it off. Personal space was sacred on the *Griffin*. She wasn't used to the casual contact allowed on the *Aegea*.

"I saw our thieves," Irina explained. "Giant spiders or beetles. They had eight legs but the bodies looked long." She couldn't repress one last shudder.

"Spiders?" he repeated blankly. "We don't have an infestation."

"You've got something. I only saw five, but there's probably more."

"Where? Show me."

Irina rubbed her neck and took a swig from her water bottle. Oh, how much she did not want to go back in there. "They've hidden themselves well. I suspect they'll have to send biologists from the zoo to identify and remove them. But, oh hell, I guess I need to show you. I probably need corroboration. Can you leave the mouth unprotected for half an hour?"

"As long as we're inside." He gathered his tablet and slid it into his own knapsack.

The immediate chamber in the labyrinth was twice the width of the rest of it. Mauricio stretched upward but then grinned and gestured to the top of the doorway. "Would you tug that screen down?"

Her insistent tug brought down a heavy-duty mesh screen. It clicked into a channel on the floor, and a red light lit on the wall.

"Are we locked in?" Irina brushed a spray of ivy off the light. This place just got worse and worse. By the end of the night, she might be happy to get kicked off this ship.

"No, it's always open from the inside. It'll prevent anyone coming in on us. Except people with the code."

Irina took a deep breath. Back into this rabbit hole then.

"Captain's going to be furious about an infestation." Mauricio led off into the first narrow corridor.

Irina silently thanked him for not making her go first. "I guess your ship will have to do a purge."

"It's your ship now too." He glanced over his shoulder at her. "Unless these beasts change your mind."

"They almost might. You haven't seen them yet."

He sighed. "When this news spreads, I bet ninety percent of the applicants for the *Aegea* will hedge off. It'll change all the lists. Even the arrangement for the Rumians." His shoulders twitched in the dim light as he walked. "I wonder who would want that?"

Irina eyed the dark strands of denuded tomato plants. "You think someone purposely introduced the spiders here?"

"It's possible." He counted on his fingers. "First, there's people who want a transfer to the *Aegea* and can't get one. Second, there's other admin who aren't getting the pool of candidates they want. Third, possible grudges against the *Aegea*?"

"I wouldn't rule out straight-up vandalism either," Irina said. "Or even terrorism."

Mauricio wobbled his head equivocally. "But we're so close to Sirius. Surely terrorism or sabotage wouldn't be…"

"There's never a time people aren't crazy." Irina knew that well. "But I admit self-interest is more likely."

"After you show me, I'll call up a list of everyone who's been escorted into the labyrinth. It's less than you'd think. Most outsiders don't want to go in."

"Imagine that. Do you think you can figure it out tonight?"

"Well, we've got six more hours. I'd rather try than just sit out there and vegetate. The real question is, who has spiders? The reported infestations are usually leaked. Everybody's heard about the rat problem on the *Necklace* and the slugs on *Thun Phu*. No one has admitted to spiders."

"Besides the regular livestock, we have a colony of fruit bats on the *Griffin*. Pollinators, not an infestation," Irina added. "I assume the zoo on the *Necklace* has insects... but that seems too obvious."

Mauricio slowed as they came to a particularly dark patch in the leafy corridor. Only a few brilliant bits of green leaf showed where the LEDs were hidden. "You realize, if these are not endemic... if they were kept secret, this is a major violation. A conspiracy even. And if they cause a panic, on top of the *Rumi* disaster..."

Irina grimaced. "Ugly."

They reached Nightmare Row too rapidly for her. This place got smaller every time she went through.

"Those five gourds." Irina pointed. "I know they look fine, but... are you laughing?"

"No. Yes, a little. Sorry. When I met you, I wondered what it would take to shake your poise. Didn't think I'd find out so fast."

"How wonderful for you. If you want to verify what I've said..."

"It wasn't an insult. Everybody has their fright. I can't stand..."

Irina threw up a hand. "I want to leave as soon as possible. So if you'll prod one of those things until you get a look, I'd appreciate it."

Mauricio tentatively swung one of them, then knocked on it politely. Irina rolled her eyes and he grinned at her again. "How big did you say..." he broke off to listen to a quiet clicking.

"Yes, hear that?" Irina said.

He tapped it more gingerly, keeping himself at arm's length. He even fingered the seam, which Irina could barely watch.

Eventually, he broke off the vegetable, twisting it round and round until the vine snapped, leaving a crushed, pulpy stem dangling above. He tossed it in his hands a few times and Irina backed to the far edge of the section.

"How about I stomp on it?" he offered.

"Best case scenario: you'll have a terrible mess."

Mauricio's mouth twisted uncertainly. He took a few steps away from her and then firmly whacked the squash on the straight edge of a bench.

He jumped back as he finished, and his body almost blocked Irina's view of the spider drunkenly tumbling off the bench. It clambered halfway up the wall and then fell back on the floor. It landed on its back, eight legs waving helplessly. And grotesquely.

Mauricio let out a string of shocked expletives, only half of which Irina knew. The rest must be Aegean slang.

#

The spider righted itself and this time climbed carefully onto the bench. It rocked back and forth a few times, then started up the wall. It went directly to the next hanging gourd and sliced it open.

Mauricio whistled. "Did you see that fang?"

A slurping noise followed.

"Can it possibly eat the whole interior? You'd think it'd be too much mass." As he spoke, yellowish goo dripped from the dangling spider, making a soft splat on the floor. "Never mind."

But Irina, firmly clenching her core to keep from shivering, was having another thought. "It's so ungainly. I thought it was just its species, but maybe it's not from a spike ship."

Mauricio raised his eyebrows. "Not used to our short-diameter gravity. Or maybe even our spin direction. That's a good thought. It's also not bothered by us."

"Definitely used to people," Irina admitted.

Mauricio edged closer to the spider. He raised a hand and Irina sucked in a breath when he hesitantly touched one of the spider's legs.

The spider paused, but not in a threatening way. Even Irina could tell it was not in pounce mode, but merely waiting.

Mauricio lifted his hand even higher—stretching onto his toes—and stroked the bristly carapace. The clicking noise started louder than ever. It made Irina jerk, but Mauricio held still. The spider twisted around and gently crawled onto his arm. Irina watched through slitted eyes, barely breathing.

Mauricio held still as it reached his shoulder. The clicking kept going, friendly and… lonely? Mauricio patted it wonderingly.

"I think…what if it's a pet?" he said.

"Ugh."

"I mean it. It's a fascinating creature, and it's almost purring."

"Who would sneak a pet like that on this ship? Who would even want…"

Their eyes met and Irina could tell they'd had the same thought.

"The kids," she said.

"From the *Rumi*." He stretched out his arm and the spider obediently climbed back up and resumed hollowing.

Mauricio pulled out his tablet and to the messy sound of slurping and splatting, they looked at the list.

The survivors of the *Rumi* medical disaster were mainly kids. Eighty had already been resettled with foster families on the *Aegea*. Five of them had made special requests to visit the labyrinth. It had been immediately granted; who didn't feel awful for these kids who'd survived their parents' death and the crippling difficulties of finishing the voyage with a skeleton crew?

"But weren't they… checked? Searched?" Irina protested.

"They were all medically cleared on the *Rumi*. I suppose they were allowed to bring personal belongings…"

Irina nodded slowly. "The spiders could have been hidden anywhere after the initial check. In a teddy bear. Rolled in a pair of pants."

It was still just a theory, but Irina felt the *fit*, the settling she sometimes got when she found an answer.

But she didn't feel relieved. In fact, she felt a sense of dread worse than before.

There were nearly five hundred kids from the *Rumi*. How many spider pets could they have had? How many ships were the spiders already on? How fast could they lay eggs?

And, this was the real dread, what kind of backlash would this draw down on those kids?

Mauricio must have been thinking something similar. "They won't be punished, surely. The *Rumi* was in disarray. They should have declared the spiders, but kids can be secretive, especially when they've suffered."

Mauricio seemed like a good guy. He certainly was ready to sympathize with these kids despite the mess they'd caused.

But somehow he didn't have any idea how much anger people could direct at kids if they felt justified. And people were so on *edge* at the moment. She'd even heard that there would be deterrence hearings for the children of the scientists who inadvertently caused the *Rumi* disaster. Deterrence, as in the courts would punish the kids for the sins of the parents, in order to prevent anyone else taking illegal risks. At the worst level, they might even sterilize them. There was no greater punishment than ending a family line before the colonization of Sirius.

This spider thing… it wouldn't be a sterilization matter, at least. But people would be furious at the risk. They'd take it out on the kids.

Suspicion, dislike, contempt.

She could hear the name calling.

Spiderspawn, arachkids, freaks.

And the spiders would mostly be killed, if there were more. The biologists might let a subset into the zoo on the *Necklace*, but if there were many, they'd be exterminated. Or left to starve, freeze, and sublimate on the *Rumi*.

Irina looked back at the spider. It was half inside the gourd now. It was disgusting, but was it some kid's lifeline?

She had to know. Tomorrow this story would explode beyond all influence of hers.

"I'm going to see those five kids. Tonight. Can you send me their flat numbers?"

"You want to find out how many more there are? You think they'll tell you?"

"Maybe. Probably. I can be intimidating."

"To what end?" The spider was almost completely inside his new home now. The occasional yellow pulp squirted out like tobacco spit.

"What if there's not more? Or… only a few? We could collect them all. Put them back on the *Rumi* and let the kids tell the officials the right way. Maybe we could get them labelled therapy animals, or perhaps they could be trained… like the bats."

"And I stupidly pegged you as a 'by the book' officer." He winced. "You realize how big a deal it would be if we cover this up? What if they already laid eggs?"

"I thought of that. We should know by the end of the Pause. If there's the least sign we missed some, I'll confess the whole thing.

You won't be implicated at all."

"The heck I won't. There's still the labyrinth damage to explain."

"Inexplicable. People won't care so much once it stops. Plus they'll be distracted by the *legitimate* and *safe* request of the children to bring new animals onto the Diadem. If I have to confess, just say you stayed outside the labyrinth. I lied and never told you what I found."

"They'll kick you back to the *Griffin*. At best. At worst…"

"I know."

"It's worth it to you?"

Irina pictured going back to the *Griffin*, for twenty long, tiring, and lonely years. Or worse, the long-term prison on the *Necklace*. She pictured the little girl's limp hands and old eyes. If these kids faced even more trauma… "Yes, it is."

Mauricio nodded. "Alright. Let's go. I know a guy who might even operate the slide carriages for us during off hours, let us back onto the *Rumi* before morning."

He twisted the gourds free, one after another. He slid three into his knapsack; it bulged, but fit.

Two went into Irina's bag. It caused her no small twinge to settle it on her shoulder.

Mauricio squeezed her arm and this time she didn't shake him off. "Unflappable," he said. "We've got five hours. Let's see how much mess we can undo before morning."

Outside the labyrinth, they looked back through the mesh. Mauricio hitched up his knapsack with one hand. "If this fails miserably, I'm gonna miss this place. It's the smell of home."

Irina hesitated, and then put her hand on his. She didn't know what to say, how to express her appreciation for his help, when he barely knew her.

He smiled and twisted his hand to squeeze her fingers. "And if this doesn't fail miserably, maybe you'll come back here when more grapes have come in. Maybe you'd come back with me?"

Irina tugged her hand free. "I was trying to say thank you, not propose. Let's see if we can't repatriate these things."

"Right. I'll ask again when you don't have spiders on your back. It's off-putting. I'm conscious of it myself."

Irina laughed despite everything.

Their footsteps echoed quietly down the corridor and the spiders clicked inquisitively from their sacks.

-o-

Corrie Garrett lives in the sunny Los Angeles area with her husband and four kids. She loves classic science fiction, from Isaac Asimov to Andre Norton, and enjoys writing science fiction and fantasy with an old-school vibe and a bit of romance. She is the author of the Alien Cadet trilogy and several stand-alone science fiction and romance novels.

Homepage: **https://corriegarrett.wordpress.com**
Mailing List: **https://corriegarrett.wordpress.com/cadet-mailing-list**

Conclusion

I hope you enjoyed this selection of stories, and that it prompted you to further explore the writing of the authors whose work was represented here.

The Officer is part of a series of science fiction anthologies. Please check out the series page at:

http://www.alasdairshaw.co.uk/thenewcomer.

We would all appreciate a review, though fully understand if you don't have the time.

You can also follow the anthology series on Facebook:

https://www.facebook.com/thenewcomerscifi.